HAUNTED HOLIDAYS

3 SHORT TALES OF TERROR

Published by GALLOWSTREE PRESS

eBook ISBN: 978-0-9850678-5-4
Print ISBN: 978-0-9850678-6-1

"The Christmas Ornament" copyright 2014 by Carolyn Haines
"The Christmas Gnome" copyright 2014 by Laura Benedict
"The Christmas Spirit" copyright 2014 by Lisa Morton

Excerpts from THE DARKLING and BLISS HOUSE used with permission from PEGASUS BOOKS LLC

Excerpt from THE DEVIL'S BIRTHDAY used with permission from BAD MOON BOOKS

Cover design by Rick Pickman

Interior and Formatting by Jennifer Talty

HAUNTED HOLIDAYS
3 SHORT TALES OF TERROR

CAROLYN HAINES
LAURA BENEDICT
LISA MORTON

DEDICATION

Endless thanks to Maggie Caldwell, P.K. Bhakta, and
J.T. Ellison

TABLE OF CONTENTS

THE CHRISTMAS ORNAMENT

by

CAROLYN HAINES (R.B. CHESTERTON)

"GATHER ROUND, GATHER ROUND." Carlos Ard waved us in closer to the fire burning in the enormous fireplace. It was, literally, big enough to roast a pig. Thank goodness Carlos had settled for some impressive logs from the woodshed rather than a hog carcass. "Since we're all waifs and orphans for the holiday season, I thought we'd celebrate in the Victorian style."

"Oh, fuck off, you insufferable nerd," Ginny Loper said, but her smile took the sting out of her words. "What are we going to do, eat sugar plums and put out milk and cookies for old Saint Nick?"

A slow smile crept over Carlos's face. "Saint Nick. You know Nick is a term for the devil, which plays very well into my Victorian evening."

Ginny stretched, the tail of her shirt lifting high above the navel ring that glittered in the light of the fire. "It's almost midnight and if we don't go to bed, Santa Claus

1

won't bring our presents."

"Oh, I'm going to give you a present," Thomas, her boyfriend said.

We laughed. We'd had too much to eat and drink and the last hours of Christmas Eve were upon the six of us. We were all graduate students in the literature program at Cornell University, all students from broken homes or parents who were MIA or dead. Not a one of us had a Christmas destination. No grandparents or aunts and uncles eagerly awaiting our arrival to share the roasted turkey and open the presents beneath a gaily-decorated tree. None of that. So we'd accepted Carlos's invitation to spend the holiday at his great-uncle's cabin in the hills near Aurora, about an hour's drive from the school.

Cabin was a misnomer. The house was huge and in good repair, though cold since there was no central heat. It was a creepy old place that sat on top of a snow-covered hill with a sharp drop-off in the back that gave onto one of the gorges so famous in this area. We'd arrived just after lunch and I'd had a chance to walk around the grounds, all wooded and quiet with three inches of snow. Breathtaking would describe the house and grounds, except for the fact that the word isolated figured prominently into the description too. I'd expected a small, intimate cabin where outdoorsmen gathered of an evening. What I'd gotten was something out of the 19th Century with gloomy, dark rooms filled with the heads—and a few bodies—of dead animals. The house rambled up three stories and sprawled across eight thousand square feet, at least.

After our dinner, we'd gathered in the large den and stayed there. Numerous bedrooms awaited, but so far, we'd made it no farther than the kitchen and the den. To be honest, the house was a bit intimidating, all dark paneling and dense shadows. It didn't invite exploration.

Carlos had waved the poor dead animals away explaining that his uncle had been a contemporary of Teddy Roosevelt and had loved safaris. "Killing was a testament to his manhood," Carlos said. "Uncle Ray-ray had some issues in that area, and killing the dangerous beasties kept the gossip down. Of course he never produced an heir."

The fire snapped and popped and the weight of all the food I'd eaten made me want to nap, but Carlos had determined otherwise. He'd planned the evening with great care.

"We're going to bring back the Victorian tradition of ghost stories on Christmas Eve," he said. "What a perfect night for it. We're virtually snowed in here. The nearest neighbors are miles away. Perfect for a little scare."

"Couldn't we just sing Christmas carols?" Ginny asked. "I don't like to be scared."

"If you wanted to sing carols you should have stayed at Cornell and gone to church," Carlos snapped. It miffed him whenever anyone tried to escape his "direction." It wasn't worth the grief to upset him. If he wanted ghost stories, I could listen.

"Why don't you tell us a ghost story," I suggested. Once he had his way, he'd forget about it and move on to something else. Still, Ginny's angry glare was as effective as a physical blow. She didn't like me. Thomas and I had dated before he started seeing her. We'd had one hot, six-week fling before I noticed he was a total narcissist. I'd extricated myself as quickly as possible and vowed never to involve myself with another graduate student. The affair was over, and we'd remained friendly, a concept Ginny had difficulty understanding since she burned every bridge she'd ever stood on.

"You sit here and listen to ghost stories, Clair. Ginny doesn't want to be scared and I want to get laid." Thomas stood up and offered his hand to his girl. She giggled and let him pull her to her feet. "How about we check out one of those upstairs bedrooms? Leave the old maids to scare themselves with tales from the crypt down here. Let's find a bed. We can keep each other warm."

3

"See you later," Ginny said, holding tight to his hand as he led her out of the room and up the creaking stairs.

"They'll be back," Carlos said. "Now, let's gather round the fire. Who wants to go first?"

I wasn't the sort to share Christmas stories—scary or otherwise—but Carlos was relentless. Once he decided on a course of action, we would fall into line or be ceaselessly badgered. I was still a bit stunned that he'd allowed Thomas and Ginny to leave the room.

"I don't really know any ghost stories, but I can give it a real Victorian twist and condense the Dickens masterpiece," I said.

"Brava! That's a wonderful beginning," Carlos said. "A nod to the master."

"Gender correct, even in your Italian." I couldn't help gigging Carlos. He could be horridly pretentious. Why I'd agreed to come to the backside of the foothills with a controlling ass, my ex-boyfriend, and his new girl toy, I couldn't fathom. But here I was and intended to make the best of it. Tomorrow, we'd all chip in cooking the Christmas dinner and then the next morning drive back to the university. I already counted the minutes.

"Spew us with Dickens," Angela Posting said. She finished a snifter of brandy and by the slightly unfocused nature of her eyes, I expected her to fall over and snore without warning. Her officemate and friend, Cecilia, was the soberest—and most uncomfortable—of all the guests. She watched Carlos as if she expected him to bite. Perhaps she wasn't far off the mark on that.

Holding my glass of brandy, I went through Scrooge and the ghosts of Christmas past, present, and future and ended with Scrooge's conversion to all things good and holy. There were a few moments when I had the audience in the palm of my hand. As I expected, Carlos wasn't greatly impressed.

Angela had no story to tell and her coherence was deeply in question, so Carlos didn't push it. Cecilia stumbled through a rendition of a family ghost story that was neither scary nor about Christmas.

At last we arrived at the moment Carlos had designed the evening around. He would tell his story. To my surprise, Ginny and Thomas reappeared at the second floor indoor balcony. Ginny was pale, and Thomas didn't look in the pink of health.

"Finished already?" Carlos asked.

"Man, there's something up there moving around. It was, like, right outside the bedroom door. Freaked Ginny out. She wouldn't stay in bed."

"A squirrel in the attic." Carlos held up the brandy bottle. "Come join us. We're creating our own literary Christmas tradition."

Ginny looked uncomfortable, but she came down the steps shivering. I couldn't help but notice her shirt was buttoned wrong. That wasn't surprising, but their reappearance in the den was. Thomas didn't really care for Carlos. He was here because Ginny wanted to go hiking tomorrow. An avid outdoorswoman, she'd brought cross-country skies, layered clothing, insulated boots, and gear that took up more than half the baggage space in the SUV we all arrived in. Carlos had convinced her that she could hike all morning and enjoy the area while we cooked. Now I could see she regretted her decision to attend the holiday gathering.

Thomas took a snifter, carefully avoiding eye contact with me. Did he feel a pang at what had changed between us? A better question was why that amused me. We'd parted with mutual desire to do so. While I could label him a narcissist, I had to admit that I'd used him, too. I'd been lonely, and he'd been available.

"This is a tale about a Christmas ornament," Carlos began. "One with a very dark past." He got up and went to a shelf. From behind some books he brought forth a red velvet box. "In our family, we stopped putting up a Christmas tree the year the house caught on fire and burned down. My family barely escaped with our lives."

He had our attention. The only sound in the room was the crackle of the fire.

Carlos put the box down on the cedar coffee table. The rich texture of the velvet seemed to catch the firelight and drink it in.

"We lost everything, except this one ornament. An heirloom from my mother's family."

"How did you manage to save it?" Ginny asked. "I mean if my house was on fire, a Christmas ornament would be the last thing I'd grab."

"I don't think my mother actually retrieved it. We found it later, on the sidewalk, safely in the box."

If Carlos was going for creepy, his words were having the desired effect. I moved a little closer to the fire but tried not to get close to the velvet box.

"Open it," Thomas said. "Let's see this ornament."

"Before I do, you should know the full story. Then you can decide if you want to see it or not. The same proposition was put to my mother when the box came into her possession. I think, if she were able, she'd make a difference decision today."

"Very funny," Ginny said. "You're just trying to scare us."

"Yes, I am." Carlos grinned and the firelight cast harsh shadows on his face, distorting his features beyond recognition.

"Let's not do this." I had a premonition that bad things might happen if Carlos opened the box. If I was a victim of his Christmas Eve ghost story, I didn't care. "Put it back, Carlos. Let's just do something else. What about cards?" I stood.

"Sit down."

I remained standing. Carlos voice still echoed in the room when something shuffled on the second floor.

"What was that?" Cecilia asked. She burrowed deeper into her jacket. "Did anyone hear it?"

"I did," went around the room. Only Carlos didn't speak.

"Is there someone upstairs?" Thomas asked. "Ginny and I heard something too. Is this some sick prank?"

"Only my dear, dead mother haunts the upper hallways," Carlos answered. He deadpanned it, which made Cecilia gasp.

"He's messing with you, stupid," Ginny said. "Don't give him the satisfaction."

"What did you hear upstairs?" I asked.

She shrugged. "We thought we heard something sliding along the hallway. It's cold up there. That's why we came back down."

"Carlos, if there's someone up there, just tell us. This may be an elaborate trick that you find amusing, but it's making the rest of us uncomfortable."

"Don't be absurd. We all arrived here together. The house was locked tight. It's an old house, creaking and shifting is par for the course. You're just a bunch of pussies afraid of your own shadows."

I wasn't satisfied, but I let it go. Carlos was the senior graduate assistant in the department. He'd been in the program for two years, three semesters longer than the rest of us. His professors spoke highly of him and entrusted him with chores the rest of us underlings weren't fit to perform. Carlos was smart, and he parroted back the premises and theses his professors promoted. He curried favor and never failed to say yes. He knew the value of a good ego-stroking.

But I'd detected a streak of cruelty. He belittled students and cut down the younger grad students whenever possible. He'd developed an elitist attitude that everyone magically bought into. Except me. The other grad students hated him for it, but they sought his favor, despite their anger, just as he did with his superiors. He ground his boot heel into the younger grad students and they licked his foot.

"Sit down, Clair." Carlos expected to be obeyed. "I'll continue with my story."

I dropped back into the sofa. If everyone else was conceding to the bully, I didn't stand a chance of stopping this freak show. I'd been insane and lonely to come up here. When I got back to campus I'd book an appointment with one of the university's free therapists. I obviously needed help. A lot of help.

"Get on with it, then," Thomas said irritably. He picked up the brandy decanter and poured a large measure into his snifter. He rolled it around as if he'd been born to the manor. What had I ever seen in him? He was as full of himself as Carlos.

"That last Christmas, after my mother found this ornament, she said it was something brought from the old country and passed down for generations."

"What old country? Transylvania?" Ginny poured more brandy for herself. She was competitive like that.

"Romania," Carlos said. "My mother was a Beswick. Marcella Beswick, a Romany. She had Gypsy blood."

The soft shuffle of footsteps overhead stopped any questions. No matter what Carlos said, there was someone upstairs. I had no doubt that when we went to our respective rooms, this hidden person would jump out and scare the wits out of us. Carlos would rush back to the school and tell all the professors how he'd frightened us. We'd be the laughing stock of the English department.

"Look, tell the story already." Angela wasn't sober, but even she was tired of the melodrama.

"Let's have another round of drinks," Carlos suggested.

I went outside on the porch and lit a cigarette. I didn't want another drink. I wanted to transport myself back to campus and my dumpy apartment. Dusk had fallen and night prepared to settle over the house and surrounding woods. In the distance I could hear a waterfall. The gorges and lakes of the area graphed the slow movement of glaciers centuries before. In better company, I would have loved this place.

More snow had fallen during the afternoon, and the landscape was stark black trees and white ground. I'd been a fool to come here without my own transportation. Now I was stuck until the day after Christmas. We were all victims of Carlos's whims.

The door opened behind me. Cecilia came out. "Carlos wants to start with the story. He asked you to come inside."

I didn't want to, but it was futile to object. "Okay. Let me finish my smoke."

She went back in and I inhaled, the tip burning bright in the gloom. I let the smoke out and bent to crush out the ember. Something moved in the tree line. For a brief moment, I thought I saw a woman standing at the edge of the trees. She wore a long black dress that blew in a gust of wind. She disappeared the instant I saw her.

Great. Now I was seeing things—the perfect patsy for Carlos and his stupid ghost stories.

Reluctant though I was, I returned to the den and the welcome warmth of the fire. I would sit and not listen. It was a childish, silly rebellion, but Carlos's constant bossing and badgering excited my inner child. I'd grown up in a house where no one considered my feelings. Ever. And I consistently placed myself in such situations over and over. Thomas, my ex, was a prime example of that. Needy, bossy, macho when everything else failed—Ginny was welcome to him.

I scanned the empty tree line one more time before I went back inside.

"The outlier returns," Carlos said, pointing to my former seat on the sofa. I took it without dissent. I would simply think about something more pleasant than Carlos's evil story. I would not allow him to frighten me or rouse my dark imagination.

"Open the damn box," Thomas said, pointing at the ornament case. "Enough is enough. You've hamboned it

9

for half an hour now."

"In good time." Carlos picked up the box. "Once opened, then the curse is let loose. Shall I open it?"

"No." Cecilia stood up. "I don't like this. I don't want to be scared. I don't want to see the ornament. I'm going to bed."

Carlos said nothing as she grabbed her backpack and headed up the stairs. "Take any bedroom you wish," he called after her. When she was gone, he glanced around the room. "First victim."

It was meant to be funny, but no one laughed.

Carlos spun his tale and despite my vow, I found myself listening to the story of the ornament. The Beswick family had practiced the art of glass blowing. Paul Beswick had been a master, creating glass sculptures valued and collected across Europe. It was a skill that saved his life when the Nazis brought death camps and destruction to the Romany people.

Despite his bullying, Carlos was a polished storyteller. He had a sense of cadence and rhythm, and he watched his audience, drawing us in, paying out the little details.

"Paul Beswick died in a death camp. It was the last act of a cruel Nazi, who knew the war had ended. He executed my forefather so that no one else would benefit from the beauty of his creations."

I didn't believe a minute of the story, but Carlos's words raised goose bumps on my arms and back.

Carlos sipped his brandy. "Paul created a number of exquisite pieces, but the one that meant the most to him was a Christmas ornament. In his pain and suffering and despair, he blew and molded the glass into such beauty that no one could resist it. Entwined with the hot, colorful glass was all of his anger and frustration. In effect, Paul cursed the ornament and any person who possessed it."

Thomas reached for the brandy bottle and I pushed my glass forward for a refill. As much as I dreaded hearing his story, I had to get to the end. I might as well enjoy a drink as I listened.

"If the Nazis had it, how did it come back to your family's possession?" Ginny asked.

"Before he was murdered by the S.S., Paul gave the ornament to the head doctor at the death camp. This was a man who'd tormented women and children with his grisly experiments. Two of those poor souls were Paul's wife and ten-year-old son. She'd died after a hysterectomy without anesthesia and the child had died when both legs were amputated above the knees. The doctor was only too glad to reveal the details of his family's suffering to Paul."

Carlos sipped his brandy and the clock in the hallway ticked and ticked, the hours of Christmas Eve slipped away.

"That doctor was found Christmas morning with his eyes and fingers removed, just as he'd done to some of the prisoners. He lived for an excruciating six days, trying to convince anyone who came into his room that he'd been admiring a beautiful ornament when he saw someone inside the glass decoration. That someone had come out and mutilated him.

"Of course no one believed him. Especially when he insisted that the person inside the ornament cut out the doctor's eyes—or so the poor deluded man insisted."

Angela twisted the hem of her shirt. She was miserable and too mousey to speak up. She should have left with Cecilia, but she didn't want to piss off Carlos.

Clearing his throat, Carlos continued. "The only signs of an intruder were drag marks on the wood and carpet, as if something wet had come inside and slithered along the floor to the bedside. One maid, who was later gassed because of possible collusion with the murderer, confessed to seeing a woman dressed in black standing near some shrubs on the lawn. She was there and gone. Always watching. Waiting."

Fear tinged the back of my tongue with an iron taste. What had I seen at the edge of the woods? A specter, a

11

vengeful spirit, or just the shadow of a tree moving across the snow as night closed in on the manor.

A darker thought touched me and a burst of anger burned away my fear. That fucker Carlos had set all of it up. How convenient that I should see the phantom of a woman in a black dress—just as presented in his "family story." And the dragging and thumping upstairs fit a little too neatly with the slide marks of a maimed and legless child.

Carlos watched the emotions play across my features as if he could read my inner thoughts. Whatever he was thinking, he merely picked up the thread of his story. "The ornament was taken by another death camp doctor, who was found three days later after he'd bitten off his tongue and choked on his own blood.

"The mysterious deaths continued. Each Nazi who looked upon the beauty of the Christmas ornament had to claim it for his own. The dazzling beauty was irresistible. And with possession of the masterpiece came a brutal death."

"Why would you want to keep a thing like that around?" Ginny asked. "You don't even have a tree to hang it on."

"Very true," Carlos said patiently. "It was only recently that I became aware the ornament was here. Uncle Ray died only a few months ago and I came up to help clear out his belongings. I found it then." Dramatic pause. "I was here alone, but someone left it in the middle of my bed."

"Maybe we should put it in the fire," Thomas said. "I wouldn't want a possessed ornament. Let's burn it and be done."

"But you haven't seen it," Carlos said. "The claim is that anyone who looks upon it becomes obsessed with the need to have it."

"Christmas sucks and this story sucks even worse." Ginny yawned and curled up against Thomas. "Can we go to bed now?"

I almost stood up, but something kept me on the sofa. It was the whisper of a sound, the *shush-slump, shush-slump* of something moving along the floor above us. We all heard it. No one spoke a word for a full minute.

"What is that?" Ginny was at last wide-awake and not surly. "What the fuck is that?"

"Cecilia!" Angela bolted to her feet. "Cecilia!" She turned to me. "She's up there alone. With that…whatever it is. We have to help her."

"Oh, grow up," Ginny snapped. "She's probably sound asleep."

"Maybe we should check on her." I didn't like the idea of going upstairs, but Cecilia hadn't made a peep in nearly an hour. I'd expected her to come back downstairs before now. She wasn't the type to fall asleep in a strange bed in a creepy old house.

"Shouldn't we finish the story?" Carlos asked.

"Look, dude, this is like being trapped in a *Saw* movie. We can figure out that the ornament in that box is the very one cursed by your forefather. You'll open the box and we'll all see the ornament, then we'll all be obsessed with owning it and we'll start to kill each other off, mostly for your entertainment. I think we can skip those parts. I want to get up early and hike and it's after midnight." Thomas put a hand to his ear. "I don't hear those pesky reindeer either so no need to stay awake any longer."

"Well, then, I suppose we'll call it a night," Carlos said. "Tomorrow we can cut a tree and decorate it, if you'd like."

"I'm hiking," Ginny said. She uncurled and stood, pulling Thomas to his feet. Her hair swung around her face as she pulled, and the firelight caught the glitter of her earrings I'd admired earlier in the day. "Let's get some shut-eye."

Though I didn't relish the idea of a night alone in one of the big bedrooms, I couldn't very well ask Cecilia and

Angela if I could bunk in with them. I was on my own, something I should have been used to. At my apartment, it wouldn't be a problem.

We went up the wide stairs en masse, individuals peeling off as they came to the door of a room. When I entered my bedroom, I was pleasantly surprised. The room was furnished in French antiques. The high bed was filled with pillows and heavy quilts. I would be plenty warm. All I had to do was go down the hall to the bathroom and then hurry back to get under the covers. Morning would arrive soon enough.

I took my flannel pjs and trotted down the hall, toothbrush in hand. The temptation to knock on Cecilia and Angela's door almost stopped me. Maybe they'd invite me to sleep in the room with them. I got so far as to lift my fist, but a noise stopped me. Something in the room.

Shush-slump.

I didn't know either of the girls very well. I worked part time in the student center serving coffee so I didn't hang out in the graduate students' offices or attend the many student functions that mostly involved drinking beer and complaining about the faculty.

As the outsider, I was the perfect scapegoat for a joke. If they were fool enough to go along with Carlos's stupid games, I wouldn't give them the satisfaction. I half-jogged to the washroom, locked the door, and took a quick, hot shower. At least the old mausoleum had plenty of hot water.

The shower worked its magic and I got out and toweled my short, dark hair. When I went to the sink, my heart almost stopped. Someone had slipped into the bathroom and written on the mirror that was covered with steam. Enim. I tried to make a word, but nothing came to mind. Then I realized it was written backwards. *Mine.* The morons should have gone with *Redrum.* Stephen King knew a thing or two about creepy stories.

I wiped the steam away. The letters, strangely enough,

14

weren't on the surface of the glass. It was as if they'd been written from the opposite side of the mirror. I opened the door to the medicine cabinet. The only thing I found was an old razor, the kind with actual blades in it, a bottle of what looked like cough syrup with a prescription label from 1974, and an empty prescription bottle for Marcella Ard. The typed lettering was so old I couldn't make out what had once been in the bottle.

Nothing else.

I closed the cabinet door, gathered my belongings and stepped into the freezing hallway. Time for bed.

I zipped into my room, locking the door behind me. Just to be on the safe side, I used the lamp by the bed to check the room. Dreading doing it, I even checked under the bed. Something about the old house brought my childhood fears to life. The room was empty, except for me.

I crawled beneath the covers and sank into a feather mattress. I would at least be toasty warm, and the sooner I went to sleep, the sooner morning would come. Maybe Cecilia and Angela would want to leave, too, and we could convince Carlos to take us to somewhere we could catch a ride back to the university. This one night I could manage, but not another. Somehow, I'd figure a way home in the morning. For the moment, I was in a locked room with a stout door. If Carlos and the others intended to play pranks on some unwitting victim, it wouldn't be me.

That thought gave me comfort as I burrowed under the quilts and drifted to sleep.

A noise awakened me. I swam to the surface of awareness like a diver too long underwater. It took a moment for me to remember where I was and who was with me. The tip of my nose—the only portion of my body not buried in the quilts--was frozen. It had to be twenty degrees in the room. Turning on my side, I tried to go back to sleep.

Shush-slump.

The noise came down the hall.

Shush-slump. Shush-slump. Shush-slump.

Closer and closer. Though I fought hard against it, I could see the young boy, his palms reaching forward and hitting the floor. *Shush!* And then dragging his body toward his hand. *Slump.* A boy who'd once run and played with his schoolmates, now condemned to use his hands for feet and to drag himself along.

I didn't want my head filled with Carlos's bullshit. I sat up, bracing myself for the cold that almost knocked the breath out of me, found the matches and lit the lamp. I was wide-awake and my watch showed only three a.m. Another three hours until daylight. I had fallen victim to Carlos's twisted Christmas story. At least we'd thwarted the grand finale by demanding to go to bed. Carlos hadn't finished his precious story.

I could imagine him opening the velvet box to reveal a glass ball of exquisite beauty, but nothing magical or cursed. A fitting end to a Christmas holiday that had all the hallmarks of a really bad decision.

Pulling the covers up to my eyes, I watched the shadows cast by the lamp dancing against the far wall of the room. The only thing to do was go back to sleep. It was either that or lie awake for another three hours stiff with cold and anxiety. Sleep was the better choice.

I'd begun to drift away when I heard the giggle. Two giggles. Someone was out in the hall not far from the door of my room. Angela and Cecilia. They were probably making a bathroom run, one too afraid to go alone so they traveled in tandem. Actually I didn't blame them. The creepy mirror trick in the bathroom almost scared me. Almost. I wouldn't give Carlos the satisfaction.

Mine.

Did it refer to the house, to the bathroom? Carlos needed to refine his bag of tricks if he wanted to really

16

scare his houseguests.

The gigglers, rather than going down the hall to the bathroom, remained outside my door. Almost as if they were hoping to lure me out into the hall. Not a chance on that. Whatever Carlos was up to, he'd have to find another victim to scare.

I closed my eyes and willed myself to sleep. Daylight would come and I would make my escape, even if I had to walk down to the small store we'd passed on the drive up. I had about a hundred dollars in cash, money I'd planned to use for a holiday splurge. I could pay someone to drive me to civilization.

When the scratching came at my door, I was almost prepared for it.

"Angela! Cecilia! If I have to get out of this bed and come and kick your ass, I'll do it. Now let me sleep!"

My answer was a delighted, adolescent giggle. The doorknob turned slowly. Someone attempted to come into the room, but the lock held. Those two morons had bought into Carlos's game hook, line, and sinker. If I found a way home tomorrow, I had no intention of taking them with me. They could rot up here in this mausoleum filled with dead things for all I cared.

"Fuck off!" I yelled it at the door.

There was no response. At last, they'd given up and gone back to bed, or to torment a new victim.

I awoke to freezing cold and the *shush-slump* moving down the hall away from my open bedroom door. It took a moment for my situation to register. I'd been sound asleep and dreaming that I walked through corridors stained with red light. Weeping and moans echoed all around me. I walked through the shifting light, dark red, then lighter, then with an intensity of near black. My footsteps echoed, slightly louder than the cries of despair and pain.

The cold had awakened me, but I was relieved to stop the dream. Better to be cold and awake then trapped in sleep and a nightmare. When I peeked out from under the mountain of covers, I discovered the open bedroom window. It had been locked and the heavy drapes drawn before I climbed in bed. Now frigid air entered the room, and the moon cascaded through the branches of leafless trees, pooling in pale light across the bedroom floor.

Panic surged, but I beat it back. Of course Carlos had a key to every room. Of course he'd come in, peering down at me as I slept—which was by far the creepiest thing that could possibly happen in this house. He'd opened the window and made his exit, eager to make sure his sound effects frightened me.

Not so fast.

I got out of bed, pulled on my jeans, socks, boots, turtleneck and sweatshirt and headed to find Carlos. I had no idea which room was his, but I'd had it with his manipulative bullshit. If I wasn't allowed to sleep, he damn sure wasn't going to either. The one thing I didn't want to do was stumble into Thomas's and Ginny's room. Wouldn't that be the final insult to a bad holiday?

The hallway was empty, and if I'd been in a jollier mood, I might have been curious how Carlos had created the sound effects that had tormented us all evening. He'd put some work into this ghost story business. Too bad I didn't appreciate being manipulated for the entertainment of a sicko. Carlos could take his Vincent Price impersonation and fuck off.

I'd taken the bedroom closest to the bath and farthest from the stairs. It stood to reason that control freak Carlos would be the first room by the stairs. As I approached the door, my nerve faltered. I could charge into the room and raise hell with Carlos for messing with me, and he would deny it. I would look like a drama queen. The grad students would tell all the professors and they would laugh behind my back.

My hand raised to knock at the door, I stopped. My watch showed four-thirty. Probably another three hours before anyone stirred. The house around me was quiet. Had I imagined the noises? Dreamed them in my red-stained palace? But I hadn't imagined the open window and door.

What if it wasn't Carlos? That deceitful, traitorous thought tumbled into my head. What if it was something else slithering around the halls seeking…what? Companionship, revenge?

Acutely aware of the darkness of the hall and the sense of emptiness around me, another fancy ripped into me. What if they'd all left? Taken the 4-wheel drive and gone down the mountain. What if I was alone in the house?

Before I even thought what I was doing, I rushed down the stairs and to the front door. A bit of warmth remained in the lower rooms, but my hands shook as I put on my coat and gloves and opened the front door. I needed a cigarette.

When I stepped onto the porch, I was met with huge flakes of falling snow. There was no sound, as if the flakes had covered and suffocated any living thing that might make noise. It occurred to me that the snow was a silent death of sorts. Whatever was alive and in the woods had been forced into burrows or hidey holes. To my relief, the SUV was parked where we'd left it, the snow piled on the hood and roof showing it hadn't moved.

I lit my cigarette and cowered against the brick of the house as I smoked.

The snow had been coming down for a while, the accumulation nearly seven inches at the edge of the porch. It was possible we'd be snowed in. The idea was completely unacceptable, but there was little I could do to change the weather.

I crushed out the cigarette and went back inside. The bottle of brandy had been left by the big fireplace in the den, and I went there for another drink. Staying sober was

19

CAROLYN HAINES

out of the question. The embers of the fire were, remarkably, still alive and I put on another log. At least I could be warm.

When I reached for the brandy, I saw the velvet ornament box. Carlos's family heirloom was sitting in the middle of the coffee table. Carlos wasn't around to stop me. I could open the box and gaze upon this wonder of blown glass and Nazi curses. As I reached for it, I saw an earring beside the box. Ginny's earring. I had commented on them earlier in the day. Topaz and turquoise.

I picked up the earring, stopped by some gross material that clung to it. Nasty, some? Ginny needed to work on her hygiene. I dropped the nasty thing on top of the velvet box. She'd had both earrings on when she and Thomas left to go to bed. I had to grin. For all of their superiority, their curiosity had driven them downstairs to check out the ornament. Alas, they were mortal after all and driven to scratch the itch of Carlos's yarn.

I reached for the box.

The *shush-slump* sound came from the top of the stairs. This time I'd find the source and put an end to the stupid terrorization. Though I ran as fast as I could, I caught only a glimpse of something crawling away. *Shush-slump, shush-slump, shush-slump*—moving so quickly.

Step by step I climbed to the second floor and faced the long dark hallway. Empty. A bedroom door creaked open slowly.

Okay, I was in the game now. If I hid downstairs, I'd never hear the end of what a coward I was. The thing to do was rush the open doorway and find the person Carlos had paid to scare us. Shush-slump my ass.

I started down the wood-paneled corridor and entered the darkened bedroom before I could think about what I was doing. As my eyes adjusted to the total darkness, something slithered across the floor and under the empty bed.

A cold lamp sat beside the bed, just as in my room. I

found the matches and lit the wick. The glass shield stabilized the flickering flame and I held the lamp up high. The first thing I saw was a turquoise and topaz earring that matched the one in the den. This was Ginny's and Thomas's room, but they weren't here.

Thomas's jeans were crumpled on top of his boots on the floor. I looked around the room and found his shirt and jacket draped over an old rocking chair. Ginny's clothes and boots were at the foot of the bed. Their suitcases remained packed in a corner,

The room contained no closets, so whatever I'd seen had to be under the bed. I steeled myself to look. Nothing.

I let out a long breath. I could easily believe that Thomas and Ginny were neck deep in the business of playing tricks on the rest of us. What I couldn't buy was that they'd do it naked in the freezing house. The possibility that perhaps Ginny and Thomas had not left the bed of their own volition touched me with dread.

The room offered no additional clues. I backed out, afraid of what might rush out of the shadows if I weren't vigilant.

I had to wake Carlos. If Ginny and Thomas were missing, he had to be notified. If it was a joke, then I was beyond caring if I was named the butt of it. I walked down the hall, my boots clacking softly on the hard wood. I tapped softly.

"Carlos?"

I thought I heard voices. So Ginny and Thomas were with him. Time to call them out. I knocked harder. "Carlos!" I'd had it. "Carlos!" I pounded on the door.

The voices grew louder, then stopped. The door opened of its own volition.

My impulse was to run away, but anger drove me forward. The first thing I felt was the heat. A crackling fire burned in the fireplace, casting dancing shadows all around the room. I stepped inside and closed the door to keep the heat from escaping. I was freezing, and the fire was deliciously warm.

The bed was lumped with quilts and pillows, but there was no dark hair in evidence. I threw back the covers to make certain Carlos wasn't hiding. He wasn't in his bed. No one else was in the room. The sound of voices must have come from somewhere else in the house, an acoustical trick of an old, drafty place.

As much as I wanted to remain beside the fire, unease sent me back into the hallway. The bedroom Cecilia and Angela had chosen was near the end of the hall, across and a little down from my bedroom. I went to their door and knocked. I might be able to enlist their help in finding Carlos, Ginny, and Thomas.

When they didn't answer, I knocked harder. What sounded like a muffled scream came from the room. I tried the door but it was locked. "Angela! Cecilia! Open the door."

"Help!"

The word was clear—there was no misunderstanding. One of the girls called out for help.

"Open the door!" I used my shoulder to try to force the lock but I wasn't strong enough.

"Clair."

My name tumbled hollowly down the hallway. I looked toward the stairs, but no one was there. I whirled to look toward the bathroom, but that was empty too.

"Clair."

"Carlos!" I yelled his name. Whatever was going on in the house, I didn't care if I became the fool, the person who lost her shit and got scared. "Where is everyone? Who's calling my name?"

I tried the door one more time and then broke and ran for the stairs. Thundering to the first floor, I raced to the den where the log still burned. The fire crackled merrily. It took me a moment to notice Carlos in a chair facing the fire. His dark hair was tousled, and he stared into the flames, ignoring my approach.

"Where the fuck is everyone?" I stood in front of him, my back to the fireplace.

He touched the velvet ornament box in his lap. "I warned them what would happen."

"What happened?"

He held the box up slightly. "They looked. Our friends couldn't resist slipping down here to peek. It's human nature, isn't it? I warned them and they looked anyway. You're the last. The hold out. I knew it would be like this."

"What do you mean?" I felt the icy tip of dread trace down my spine. Carlos was insane. I should have seen it before now. He looked up at me, his skin warmed by the fire and a sleepy smile on his face.

"Merry Christmas, Clair."

"Where are the others?" I wanted to punch him, to tear his hair and kick him, anything to force him to tell me the truth. "Where are they?"

"Gone."

"They can't just be gone. The car is here. Their things are here."

He nodded, as if someone else talked to him. "Yes, gone. It can't be helped. I know. They're gone."

"Carlos!" My voice cracked. "Where are the others?"

The lethargy wore away, little by little. Sharpness returned to his dark eyes. "Clair," he said. "What are you doing up?"

"The others are missing. They aren't in their rooms. We have to find them."

He shook his head. "Wouldn't you like to see the ornament? It's a family heirloom."

"What I'd like is to find the others and go back to Cornell."

"They're gone."

Circular logic, one of the things Carlos argued so vehemently against in the classes he taught. "Gone where?"

He shook the box. "In here."

23

I knew what he was saying, but I couldn't grasp his meaning. "They went into the box?"

"The best part of them."

The *shush-slump* noise came from upstairs again.

He looked up. "The rest of them, what's left, that's all in the kitchen."

The fire had warmed the back of my legs until my jeans were red hot against my skin. I had to step away from the fire.

"Come with me to the kitchen." The fear that if I left him, he too would disappear, was too strong to ignore.

He stood up like a sleepwalker. "I didn't want to do this. I had my plans. I'm only a semester away from my degree, and I have a job offer from a college in Pennsylvania for next fall."

I had no clue what he was babbling about. I grabbed the sleeve of his shirt and dragged him behind me. With each step, my dread of the kitchen took a firmer hold. Something, a soft murmur of voices, filtered to me. I couldn't make out the words.

"Who's here with us?"

"They made me do this. I found the ornament and looked. I didn't know. The only way to save myself was to bring others."

I wheeled around and slapped him with all of my might. "Stop fucking babbling like a moron and tell me what happened."

The light of intelligence in his eyes dimmed into emptiness. I tugged his sleeve and he followed like an obedient zombie. At the closed door to the kitchen, I stopped.

The conversation also stopped. Behind me, Carlos began to moan softly. "I had to do it. I had to."

I wanted to kill him but then I'd be alone. A babbling idiot was better than alone. I pushed open the door.

The little boy stood facing me at the door. He wore dated clothes, and something wasn't right about him. My glance swept to the stove where a woman in a black dress stirred a pot. The scent of baking bread came from the oven.

The bodies of my friends slumped around the table. Ginny had been gutted. Thomas had no legs. Angela and Cecilia were missing eyes and fingers.

"Clear the table, Mihai. Our guest is hungry." The woman spoke with a broken accent.

The boy stumbled and I grasped what was odd about him. His legs were wrong, the legs of a man not a child. He went to the chair closest to me and pushed Ginny to the floor. He pulled out the chair and held his hand open, inviting me to sit.

Pivoting, I ran for the door. Carlos suddenly came to life. His arms circled me, halting me from escaping. He was far stronger than I anticipated. "You can't leave," he said. "You can never leave. Neither of us."

"They're dead. They're all dead." I saw it but didn't believe it.

"I know," he whispered. "I had no choice. Nagyi and Mihai wanted to come back, to have the life that was stolen. I found the ornament and looked. I had no choice then. The ornament made it possible. I only had to find replacement parts for what had been taken from them so long ago in the death camp."

I struggled until exhaustion stilled my body. Carlos dragged me to the chair and plunked me into it.

The woman brought a plate of food and put it in front of me. Carlos shoved Thomas's legless trunk to the floor and sat. She put a plate in front of Carlos, too.

"We have practiced the English," the woman said. "Merry Christmas."

"Merry Christmas," the boy repeated.

Outside the snow began to fall again, but it didn't matter. What held me now was so much more powerful than snow.

"Merry Christmas," the woman said, this time with an

edge. Her dark eyes dared me.

"Merry Christmas," the boy echoed.

"Merry Christmas," Carlos mumbled. He nudged me under the table.

I swallowed. "Merry Christmas," I said at last.

THE CHRISTMAS GNOME

by

LAURA BENEDICT

VENUS DIDN'T HAVE TO SEE THE return address
on the package to know who sent it. Even as the postman
walked up the flagstone path from his truck, she
recognized the telltale sheen of the yards of packing tape
that had been wrapped around and around it. For all her
mother-in-law's careless housekeeping and questionable
personal hygiene, she was particular about how her gifts
traveled across the Atlantic.

"Four days after Thanksgiving, and the truck's already
full up with packages." The postman reached the porch
steps. "Hey, that's a pretty apron you're wearing, Mrs.
Hansen. Do I smell cookies?"

The postman—whose name badge read "Bev Stone"—
shifted his weight to peer into the open door behind her,
his uncombed hair falling away to expose an unnaturally
small ear with a murky diamond chip fastened in the lobe.

Bev for *Beverly*, no doubt, she'd thought on their first meeting. Her father, an astronomer, might be excused for giving his daughter a fanciful name like *Venus*, but who in the world would call their son *Beverly*? It made her feel sorry for the man. She also suspected he had a bit of a crush on her, and while she would never encourage such a thing, she certainly didn't mind that he always made sure the Hansen family mail was timely and neatly organized.

Venus wagged a chiding, manicured finger at him from the top step. "You're going to have to wait until tomorrow for those cookies, Bev. They're about to come out, but they'll be too hot."

As she took the package, she heard a voice, distant and small.

It's about damn time.

It wasn't the postman's voice, and they had no neighbors in sight.

"Did you hear that?" Venus tilted her head, listening for more.

"What? Oh wait. I need you to sign."

As Bev reached for the electronic recorder hanging at his side, Venus glanced down at the top of the package. Their mailing address was covered by the loose mail, but when she confirmed that the slanting return address was *Tromsø, Norway*, she gave a small, involuntary shake of her head.

"Is everything okay, Mrs. H?" Bev's eyes, behind his aviator-style glasses, were concerned.

Venus looked up, feeling the color rise in her face, and it was as though everything around her was more vibrant: the withered oak leaves clinging stubbornly to their branches had turned the rich color of April mud, the grass lining the front walk was less the color of hay and had turned an emerald green. A blue jay dove through the branches of the oak with an angry cry. But around the edges of her vision, everything was fading to gray.

"Steady there, Mrs. H." The postman let the scanner

dangle by its strap and took back the package so she could steady herself on the porch railing. "You should sit down. Put your head between your knees."

He tried to guide her down to sit on the step, but she pushed him away.

"No. I'm fine." She breathed deeply, the topmost part of an odd triangle highlighted in the weak November sunshine, the postman and the gleaming package sitting on the porch a couple feet away forming the other points.

When she regained her composure, she shook her head, her glossy blonde ponytail shimmying behind her, and she was once more the picture of attractive, blue-eyed, pink-cheeked young motherhood. "I must have gotten up too fast. I'm sorry."

What she said didn't make sense, but Bev had heard stranger things from pretty women before—and there were quite a few pretty, lonely mothers on his route. He didn't say, but he wondered if Venus Hansen might be pregnant. Women on television were always fainting when they got pregnant.

"You want some help inside?" It was a reasonable question, though he didn't really expect her to invite him in.

She glanced down, catching sight of his dusty brown brogues. "Just hand me the package if you would."

He came up one step to make sure she could take the package easily.

"You're so nice. Now, I'll have cookies tomorrow. So even if we don't have mail, do come by, okay?"

When the door was closed behind her, Venus carried the package to the kitchen island. In a kind of imagined race between herself and the cookies baking in the oven, she sorted through the loose envelopes, opened them, and put them in their requisite files for payment, then took the single catalog to the recycling bin in the garage. Letting the garage door close softly behind her, she smelled a hint of burning sugar and cinnamon.

Damn.
The cookies had burned.

Using a sharp paring knife, Venus carefully cut through the layers of tape sealing the top of the box.

Over the last three years, the vetting of the annual Christmas box from Helen Hansen had become her own strange, solitary tradition, done before the children even knew it had arrived. Always the boxes were full of odd surprises—things that didn't seem to be gifts so much as random objects purchased at a downscale antique mall: fragile dishes stained with food, a faded dishtowel printed with landmarks from the German Democratic Republic, a mechanical cat with directions written only in Japanese, a box of burled walnut containing the bones of some small rodent. (Steffan, her husband, had assured her that his mother had surely not even opened the walnut box before she bought it.) Last Christmas there had been an unopened moon phase poster that was two years out of date. But Venus considered herself a polite person and, no matter that her mother-in-law had never reached out in friendship to her—in fact hadn't even embraced her at her wedding to Steffan—she only complained about the gifts to her mother and closest friends after donating them to their church's thrift store. Indeed, the revelation of the contents of each year's box made for amusing coffee conversation.

Steffan usually laughed, a little embarrassed, when Venus showed him the gifts she confiscated, and was agreeable when she replaced the children's gifts—the only ones ever labeled with the recipients' names— with small toys she knew they would like. It wasn't as though Helen ever came to visit to see what had happened to the things she'd sent. And after their first and only visit to Tromsø, Venus had refused to return.

To her immense relief, there was nothing obviously

dangerous in this year's box, and, in fact, nothing had been truly dangerous since Jack, then only two years old, had eaten a handful of moldy cashews he'd found among the crumpled newspaper in the bottom of the box. (He vomited them up, but was otherwise all right.)

This year's gifts were surprisingly rational: a potholder loom set of at least a decade's vintage—but still unopened—for seven year-old Mary, and a new tube full of colorful plastic dinosaurs for Jack. Venus knew Steffan didn't care too much that his mother's boxes were always strange and disappointing (he had grown up with her and so her *surprises* weren't that surprising), but thought it would please him that this year's gifts weren't too weird or disgusting.

There was only one other gift in the box. Venus untied the ribbon securing the grubby linen bag and let it fall from the small statue inside.

It was a gnome, slightly smaller than any garden gnome she'd seen—about twelve inches tall from the heels of its black boots to its red, pointed hat. But unlike a plaster gnome, this one's conical hat was of faded red felt, and slumped, deflated across its head. It wore blue denim pants that might have been dark once, but were now covered in a kind of gray film that Venus strongly suspected was some kind of mold. Its vest was green felt—lacking seams except at the sides and across the shoulders—and was secured over a dingy lawn shirt by a row of bright gold buttons. One button was missing, but the vest and shirt appeared to have escaped the scourge of whatever film was on the pants.

The gnome's gray beard was neatly trimmed, but, like the gray hair escaping from his hat, was corded with age and grime. Its shockingly red lips curved in a stiff smile, revealing just a hint of a row of ivory-colored teeth.

"Ew."

Venus didn't much want to touch the thing, so pinched its shoulder between her thumb and middle finger to turn it around. Taped to its back with a piece of cellophane tape was a handwritten note. She bent to read it, and the words caused her brow to crease.

It was her habit—and she was definitely a woman of habit—to take anything she was planning to donate to the thrift store immediately out to the trunk of her minivan. And she did intend to donate the gnome. But that afternoon it only made it as far as one of the shelves in the mudroom, just shy of the garage door.

Where does one draw the line between accidentally forgetting to do something and accidentally forgetting *on purpose?* Venus made two trips to the thrift store in the coming weeks, even filling the box in her trunk with Christmas decorations she'd tired of, and still didn't manage to load the gnome in its linen bag into the minivan. It rested on a mudroom shelf, close to the interior door to the garage, as though it had always been there. Her eyes casually passed over it as they did over the pool toys and grill accessories that waited on the shelf for another season.

Steffan sipped a bourbon, watching Venus follow behind the kids as they crowded ornaments on the lowest branches of the Christmas tree. As always, she wore a long-sleeved sweater, hiding the marks on her wrists that were almost faded. She'd been fragile when they met, still compulsive, but recovering. He'd fallen in love with her determination to handle the nameless, crippling anxiety she'd felt for most of her life. And, to be honest, her athletic figure and bright blue eyes hadn't hurt, either.

He knew she was trying to make the kids feel better by saying things like, "Oh, let's put this one somewhere it can dangle free," and "See, if we separate these two—like this—you can see both of them!" She was right there, making sure everything was *just so*. Tonight she would be awake after everyone went to bed, rearranging, rehanging, fixing and fixing. Jack, who was six, was already taking after her. They'd discovered only the week before that he'd searched out and thrown away all the pencils that he could find in the house that had small teeth marks in them where his seven year-old sister, Mary, had chewed, thoughtfully, as she did her homework and handwriting practice. Venus had laughed, and smoothed Jack's already-smooth blonde hair, announcing that at least *somebody else* in the house cared about having nice things. He was only a little bit worried about Jack.

"Steffan, would you be a darling and get the silver icicles I bought this morning for the tree? I must not have gotten all the bags out of the van."

While he knew her need to have a lot of control over the world around her would always be a part of her, sometimes he felt like another one of her children: attractive, frequently troublesome, and occasionally useful for small tasks that made her world a more orderly, acceptable place.

Mellowed by the bourbon, he didn't bother to complain.

"What is it, Daddy? What is it?" Mary bounced in her socks, setting her coppery pigtails swinging. "Can I open the bag?"

A few feet away, Venus had her back to the rest of the family as she rinsed the mugs and plates they'd used for cocoa and cookies and loaded them into the dishwasher. They'd finished the tree and were all gathered in the kitchen. Steffan had his pocketknife out and was about to cut off the ribbon that Venus had so carefully retied.

"Grandma sent us a present from Norway. I found it in the mudroom where Mommy was hiding it as a surprise."

Was that censure in his voice? Of course she should have told him what his mother had sent, and she felt badly about it. Maybe that was why she'd never quite gotten around to donating it?

"You're not going to use a knife on it, are you?" Jack worried a lot about knives.

Steffan saw him staring at the open pocketknife in his hand.

"Well, no, I don't have to, I guess." He closed the pocketknife and stuck it in his pocket. "I'll just untie it." When he winked at Venus, she knew he wasn't too irritated with her. He—more than anyone—knew how unpleasant his mother could be.

From the beginning, Helen Hansen had been cool to her daughter-in-law and they hadn't grown closer with time. Long-divorced from Steffan's father, she'd left the states after Steffan's and Venus's wedding to move back to Tromsø, in her native Norway. There, she took an apartment with her sister, Marta.

Certain that bearing her mother-in-law a grandchild would soften the woman, Venus had agreed to go to Tromsø when Mary was a few months old. The three of them stayed in a guest room the size of Venus's current linen closet because Helen didn't *believe* in relatives staying in hotels when there was a "perfectly good" room available at the apartment.

The apartment was full of tchotchkes, mostly childish things like glass gazing balls and intricate fairy houses, carved gnomes and fairies, stuffed toy animals—wolves and bears and cats. But also wands and boxes full of stone and shell runes. Symbols and carvings Venus thought might be Celtic, and crystals. Hundreds of crystals. Over it all there was a yellow layer of grime and smoke.

Venus hadn't been to his mother's house in the states, and Steffan had certainly never had similar things in his apartment, so she found it very strange.

"I don't understand," she whispered to him when they were finally alone in their cramped bedroom. "It's like some store out of *Harry Potter*. What *is* all this stuff?" She picked up a small handful of crystals from a wooden bowl shaped like a leaf.

Steffan's handsome, fair face colored. He was blue-eyed like his wife, but his face was broader than it was long, his nose and cheekbones chiseled and sharp. He kept his straight auburn hair and beard neatly trimmed. His clean, uncluttered features were a huge attraction for Venus. She liked things around her to be straight and serious. Steffan was usually both.

"I stayed in my bedroom a lot. After my dad divorced her, she started in with this Old Ways stuff. Just don't pay any attention to it, okay?" He kissed her on the nose. "We won't be here for very long."

Helen wasn't at all moved by Venus's efforts at conversation or offers to help, and largely ignored her in favor of Steffan and Mary. There was no refuge with Aunt Marta, either, who was pleasant and smiling and nodding, but didn't speak a word of English. In fact, she barely spoke. During the visit, the two older women smoked like chimneys, their ashtrays overflowing at the end of each day, and they insisted on cooking every meal but one. By the end of their five-day visit, Venus knew she would never eat another meatball or piece of herring, and she was afraid she might never want cheese again, either.

Mary had cried almost constantly, and one afternoon Venus and Steffan returned from a quick museum visit to discover Steffan's mother funneling brandy into Mary's bottle.

Venus had lost it, and the rest of the visit was ruined for everyone.

* * * * *

"It looks like a doll! Can I have it?" Mary was excited.

Venus folded and hung up the dishtowel, and turned to see Steffan holding the gnome up to get a better look at it in the light.

"He's nice," Jack said. "Look at how he's smiling, Daddy."

The gnome *was* smiling, and Steffan found himself smiling back at the cheerful wooden face. Despite the dilapidated state of his clothing, the gnome's face wore a bright sheen of veneer over its painted features: wide, round blue eyes with long, elegant lashes below a pair of hefty salt and pepper brows that were as charmingly unkempt as an old man's might be. He was bearded, but there was a mustache above his candy-red lips. His nose was rounded and tipped with pink, just like one of Mary's expensive baby dolls. The only defect—if it could be called a defect—on the gnome's face was a fine line in the shape of an inverted crescent just below his left eye. Holding the gnome at arm's length, Steffan noticed the crescent scar had the effect of making the gnome look as though he were squinting. Steffan was put in mind of a pirate, but he didn't remember any pirates in the tales of gnomes he'd heard as a kid.

"Do you think it's one of your mother's?" Venus asked him.

"The gnome?" Steffan shook his head. "I don't remember seeing it before."

"Did Grandma send anything else?" Mary grabbed for the bag to peer inside. She pulled out the paper that had been stuck to the gnome's vest. "It's a letter. Can I read you the letter? Please, Daddy?" But Steffan wasn't listening. He was still inspecting the gnome.

"Here, darling, let Mommy have it." Venus held out her hand for the paper, but Mary wouldn't give it up.

"I can read it!"

She was a good reader and only needed a small amount of help.

"I am the Christmas Nisse
I bring your home good cheer.
I can grant your wishes
If you whisper in my ear.
Pay no mind my mischief,
A nisse will have his fun.
Feed me nuts and berries,
And I'll eat until I'm done.
Be on your best behavior,
With Julenissen I confer.
If you treat me well, my friend
Christmas favors will be yours.

"What's *confer* mean? And why doesn't it rhyme at the end?" Mary handed the poem to Venus, who folded it and tucked it into the pocket of her sweater, wondering how she could get the gnome out of the house without upsetting the children. They liked stories. Maybe she could tell them that it had gone on some kind of journey.

She heard quiet, satisfied laughter, and looked at Steffan. But he wasn't even smiling. Jack leaned against the island studying the gnome's feet. And it had definitely been a man's laughter. Unpleasant laughter. Perhaps, she thought, it was her subconscious mocking her.

"He's like the shelf elf that lives at Emily's house." Jack rubbed the tip of the gnome's boot with a finger. "That's what *mischief* means. Right, Mommy? Like how their elf knocked over Emily's detergent in the laundry room and drew pictures of a reindeer and Santa in it."

Mary giggled. "It put green and red M&Ms in everybody's shoes!"

When Steffan looked at Venus quizzically, she said, "It's a toy elf that comes with a book, and it lives at your house in the weeks before Christmas and spies on the kids

LAURA BENEDICT

and tells Santa if they're naughty or nice." She waved a dismissive hand. "It's silly."

"Mommy said our house is too nice to have elves make messes in. She says Jack and me make plenty of messes."

Steffan nodded. "I get it."

"The shelf elves start early in December, like with the Advent Calendar. It's too late, anyway." Venus pointed to the handcrafted wooden gingerbread-style house with numbered doors and windows that sat on a table near the Christmas tree. "Only four more days until Christmas."

"But wishes, Mommy! The poem says we get wishes!" It wasn't easy to get Jack excited, but now his serious blue eyes were lively with hope.

"We don't have a special Santa Claus spy. And Emily's elf is named Rodney. All my friends at school have elves." Mary's voice had tipped from merely complaining to an overt whine. "Why don't we have an elf?"

"I explained that already, Mary."

Steffan picked up the gnome again, this time holding it in both hands and tilting it from side to side as though making it dance. "Who needs an elf, when we have a gnome?" He grinned at Mary.

With that, Venus knew it was decided. Steffan would take on the role of troublesome Christmas gnome whether she liked it or not.

Venus used a tissue to wipe a smear of that morning's Advent calendar chocolate from Jack's mouth. "Run up and get whatever you want to take for show and tell." She patted him on his corduroy-covered bottom, and he ran off toward the back stairs. "Is your backpack by the door, Mary?"

"Just a minute." Mary stood looking at the scene on the coffee table in the family room. "I don't understand. Is the gnome in jail?"

Venus came to stand beside Mary.

The previous morning, she and the children had come into the kitchen to find the gnome, his feet covered in plastic wrap, standing on the kitchen island in the middle of an aluminum foil lake—maybe it was supposed to be a lake—with *Merry Xmas* written on the foil in sloppy marker, and bathed in liquid laundry detergent.

Mary had laughed so hard that she made a show of lying on the floor and rolling around until Venus had to tell her to stop. Jack had stared, perplexed.

When Steffan came down a few minutes later, he pretended surprise. "Wow. It's like he's taking a bath. Pretty cool. And it doesn't seem very messy to me at all, does it?" At this he gave Venus a *significant look.*

"The gnome doesn't look very happy." Jack fiddled with the plastic wrap around the gnome's feet. He's got goop on his beard."

"That's not goop. It's detergent," Mary said. She wrinkled her nose. "Now our breakfast is going to smell like laundry. Ew."

It was Tuesday, which was a cereal morning, so Venus took bowls from the cabinet. As she put them on the breakfast nook table, she said, "I'm afraid our gnome might not be very smart."

"What do you mean? Not smart?" Steffan sounded genuinely hurt, and Venus immediately felt sorry for making fun. "He seems perfectly smart to me. He wished us a *Merry Christmas*, and the detergent smells nice. He could have used—I don't know—vinegar. Or orange juice."

Jack shook his head solemnly. "You can't see through orange juice, Daddy. It's not transferent."

They all stared at him a moment.

"You mean *transparent*," Venus said. She smiled. It *was* pretty funny, and Steffan had worked hard not to make a mess, trying to please her. "It's just odd that our gnome used liquid detergent. The powdered kind that Emily's elf used looks like snow."

Steffan shrugged. "Snow? Oh, yeah, the North Pole thing. Well, that's a gnome for you. Contrary."

"I don't know, sweetie." Venus knelt down to examine the gnome, who was confined in an indifferently assembled collection of Jack's colorful building blocks. "It does kind of look like he's in prison." She had to give Steffan credit for originality, if not complete randomness. At least the blocks he'd chosen were green and red and white—nominally Christmas colors. And he hadn't made a mess.

"Has he been bad?" Mary touched Venus's shoulder, worried. For all her bravado, she was a well-behaved child and was as worried about being bad as Jack was about knives and getting lost. "How did he get in there? Did he build it and then climb in?"

Venus loved how smart her children were, even though it was wrong to tell them so. It was so hard to find that perfect balance between making sure they had good self-esteem and not making them conceited.

"Well he's magical, right?"

"I guess so." Mary was doubtful.

Venus suspected it wouldn't be long before Mary stopped believing in Santa Claus, which in the end would be a kind of relief. It was important for children to have fantasy in their childhood, but it couldn't last forever.

"Why don't you tell him your wish?"

Mary cast her a secretive look. "I already did," she whispered. "Do I get to tell him another one?"

"Of course." What could it hurt? Venus was certain she knew all of her children's wishes. She kept a secret list throughout the year of toys Mary and Jack mentioned.

"Go away, Mommy. I can't tell him if you don't leave. It's a secret."

Mary began to push her away even as she was rising to

her feet. Off-balance, Venus stumbled, gashing her bare leg on the corner of the glass coffee table whose rubber child-proofing corners she'd removed only a few months before.

"Ouch! Dammit!" She fell heavily onto her bottom, and quickly clamped a hand over the bleeding wound.

Mary stood wide-eyed over her for a moment, then ran to the back stairs.

"Daddy! Come here! Mommy's bleeding and she said dammit!" Not getting an immediate response, she ran up the stairs, leaving Venus to look around for something to keep the blood off of the floor.

Finally, she slipped out of her robe and wrapped it around her knee. It would be a nightmare to get the blood out, but at least she wouldn't have to clean it out of the carpet. Hobbling away toward the kitchen, where the radio was playing a Beethoven sonata, she heard a voice behind her.

Nice ass.

"He spoke to me. It was definitely him." Venus's voice shook. She tried a little laugh, to cover. "I know it sounds crazy."

Steffan had set Mary to pouring cereal, milk and juice for herself and Jack. When Venus tried to object, knowing how much milk and juice would end up on the floor, Steffan had silenced her with, "People who are bleeding don't get to make breakfast."

Now he was cleaning the gash on her leg with alcohol swabs while she sat on the closed toilet seat.

"Damn. You really got yourself, honey." He gently prodded the edge of the wound, and it began to bleed again in earnest. Her soiled robe lay on the floor by the vanity sink.

The cut burned, but not too badly. Still, she was more

concerned about what she'd heard. "Steffan, that troll told me that I have a nice ass. What the hell is that about? Did you rig it so it would talk?"

When he looked up at her and shook his slightly too-long bangs away, she couldn't tell if he was being serious or not.

"Why would I do that? Why would anybody do that?"

"That's what I want to know."

"It's a gnome, not a troll. There's a difference. In the mythology, gnomes are good. They just don't like cats."

At a cry from the kitchen, Venus started forward but Steffan pushed her back.

"You need to sit still," Steffan said. "If you don't, I'm going to sew you up right here. With regular thread." He was pressing the wound closed. Another couple of centimeters and they would've been looking at several stitches. As it was, he would tape it together with surgical butterfly bandages.

"You wouldn't," Venus said.

"You can try me."

"Really. I swear I heard him."

Steffan kissed her on the cheek. "You do have a nice ass. It's not like it's a secret."

Venus hardly recognized herself in the mirror. Her face looked pale and ghoulish, her hair, still naturally blonde enough to not require highlights, seemed lank.

Lank. An abhorrent word. A word that spoke of an absence of care and attention.

There were dark circles under her eyes, as well, from staying up too late making the stained glass Christmas candy she made every year: boiling the sugar mixture, flavoring the red with cherry, and the green with peppermint, the pink with cinnamon, and the yellow with lemon, then cooling it in large pans and using the towel-wrapped head of a hammer to break it into shining pieces that shimmered like real broken glass.

"You really didn't make him talk?" Maybe she *was* just

tired.

"No, I didn't. I promise. He didn't even answer me when I told him my wish."

Now Venus really laughed. Steffan didn't believe in anything like wishes. She could barely even get him to read a book that didn't have tables, graphs, and columns of numbers in it.

You want to know what she wished?

Before leaving for school, Mary had decided that it wasn't fair that the gnome should have to be imprisoned all day in the blocks and so had brought the gnome into the kitchen and placed him in the garden window above the sink.

The suddenness of the voice in the silent house made it somehow worse than it had been that morning, when the rest of the family was upstairs. It was a distinctly male voice, unaccented. A low, confiding, but matter-of-fact voice. It was the voice of someone who meant to be heard.

You know the one I mean. What do you call her? Mary, Mary, quite contrary.

The voice froze Venus for a moment—there was no way it was real— but she continued soaping the cookie sheet she was washing, refusing to turn her eyes to the thing. Holding the pan carefully at one end, she used the aerator wand to sluice the scalding, soapy water into the sink. As the steam rose in front of her, the water in the sink also rose. Lifting her eyes, looking past the gnome, she saw that the bottom of the window was gathering a fine layer of moisture.

Mary said she wants a doll that looks just like her and has matching pajamas.

The way he said Mary's name, drawing it out, exaggerating, made her name sound filthy in his mouth. Salacious.

She also said she wishes you'd fallen down and slit your throat on the table.

Without hesitating, Venus knocked the gnome into the steaming sink where it bobbed from side to side on its belly before resting, half-submerged among the bubbles.

Don't be grouchy. Let's have some fun today.

Venus had laid the gnome on a towel on the island to dry, but obviously his swim in the sink had had no effect on his attitude. Part of her was sure she was going insane, but another part—a seldom-acknowledged, shy part of her brain that sometimes got tired of being the practical, competent woman she was—had no problem believing in the voice at all. But that didn't mean she had to listen to everything he said. She ignored him as she made a list of the serving dishes and crystal she would need to get out for Christmas dinner. She had a vision for how she wanted the table to look, even bookmarking online table settings on her tablet. Her parents were coming, and every holiday was a chance for her to show them how truly civilized people lived. Her mother wasn't slovenly like Steffan's mother, but she definitely didn't understand that there was always a proper way to do things.

Your friend Bev is almost here. Why not invite him in for some Christmas cheer? You've already got cider warming on the stove for the kids.

"Because he's the postman." Venus surprised herself by answering. How was he talking, anyway? His mouth didn't move.

You're such a snob, Venus.

"I'm not."

His tone turned sneering. *That's what you say. So much for your gracious hostess act. I guess Helen was right about you.*

Venus put down her mechanical pencil—the one she hid from Mary and her busy teeth. "What do you mean?"

That's why she hasn't come to visit yet. She thinks you're a cold-ass cunt.

The nastiness of his words struck her. What a vile thing he was! What he was saying couldn't be true. Steffan had always said that his mother never liked any of his girlfriends, or even his friends, because she was jealous. That when he was a teenager, she never passed on their phone messages or let them come to the house. Surely, in Helen's eyes, she—Venus—was simply no different from them.

"You don't know anything."

The gnome stayed silent, chastened, she hoped. But she thought back to the notes and letters and thoughtful gifts she'd sent Helen, the cheerful telephone calls. She'd tried. Yes, she'd tried so hard to be nice. To be friendly, even in the face of Helen's coldness. Venus considered herself to be a *very* nice person, with friends. Friends who thought she was funny and generous. Now she knew the truth, though. Helen had sent the gnome to torment her.

Confident with her new knowledge, she finished up the list and went to the dining room to pull everything she would need out of the china cabinet. When it was neatly arranged on the sideboard, she went back to the kitchen to stir the stew cooking in the crockpot. So this was how much Helen hated her. She mentally kicked herself for not getting rid of the gnome when she had the chance.

He's here.

Venus looked down the hallway. Sure enough, she saw the distorted shape of the mail truck through the sidelight glass.

So, are you going to be nice to him, or what?

When Mrs. Hansen—he liked to think of her as Venus, but not when he was around her, because what if she were, by some stretch of the imagination, able to read his mind?—opened the door and came out onto the porch, she seemed to be favoring one leg over the other. Bev didn't want to be rude and ask her why. She was so pretty, though today she didn't have on her usual makeup. He hoped she wasn't sick.

At first she wasn't smiling. In fact she looked worried, but then it was almost as though a switch flicked on inside her, and she grinned and said, "Come on in. Merry almost-Christmas! I have some cider on the stove."

Bev's pasty, unshaven face colored. "We're not supposed to come inside. It's against regulations, Mrs. Hansen. He held out the banded stack of mail, but she had stepped back, holding the door open for him to follow. It was damned cold, and the wind whipped so fiercely that dried leaves skittered past him on the porch, threatening to jump the two-inch threshold of the door and get inside. And the house did smell like he always imagined Christmas should smell: cinnamon and sugar and pine. But it also smelled of Venus Hansen: fresh and a bit like oranges. And woman. Venus Hansen smelled like a woman.

"Oh, at least come in for a minute." She smiled so warmly that it lit up her blue eyes. "I'll put some in a go-cup, and get your present."

He stepped inside, and she closed the door behind him.

Because his glasses immediately steamed up, he couldn't see anything. Tucking the mail beneath one arm, he took them off and wiped them with the hem of his coat.

"Thanks," he said. "It *is* bitter today."

She gave a small, nervous laugh and hurried down the hallway.

Most of the houses on his route were nice, but he'd imagined that Venus's house would be nicer inside than the others, and he wasn't disappointed. The hallway was filled with ropes of evergreen decorated with ribbons and gold pinecones going all the way up to the railing along the second floor. There was evergreen rope, too, over the mirror, and a pair of thin, potted Christmas trees trimmed with miniature lights on a table. There was a carousel between the trees, the kind with candles whose flames would make the painted horses spin and dance. The carousel made him like Mrs. Hansen more because it reminded him of something his grandmother might have.

In front of the carousel lay a strange doll—no, it wasn't a doll, but a kind of troll or gnome, the kind you see in a garden, but much smaller. It didn't look like part of the decorations, the way it was just lying there with its hat and head sticking out in the air off the table's edge. It was old, too, and looked wet, its beard in tangled, gray curls. Was it really wet?

Bev poked at it with two fingers. Yes, the gnome's flannel vest was damp, and the poke had pushed it just enough to reveal a widening wet spot on the table's surface. That didn't seem like a good thing.

"Just a minute." Mrs. Hansen called from the kitchen. "I need to run upstairs. I'll be right down."

He listened for the presence of someone else in the house. Specifically Dr. Steffan Hansen, the other adult resident of 1964 Mockingbird Lane. The Dr. Steffan Hansen who got mail from the International Association of Otolaryngologists, Brooks Brothers, and Ducks Unlimited along with the occasional airmail envelope from Norway. Bev heard Venus Hansen moving around upstairs, and Christmas carols coming from a radio in the kitchen, but there was no Mr. Hansen. No one at all, except for Mrs. Hansen, and the children were still in school.

The thought of being alone in the house with Venus— Mrs. Hansen—made him anxious. Something rubbed inside his brain, an idea waiting to be born. An idea that made him nervous. He glanced down at the gnome. It looked back at him with round, confident eyes. But there was something in its glossy grin that made Bev think of Venus Hansen's tits. They were nice tits. Even excellent tits.

He thought often of Venus Hansen's tits and the way they pressed with gentle insistence against her clothes. He thought of filling his mouth with one of those pert, shapely tits.

Where was she? Why had she left him waiting? He looked around the heavily decorated hall. He looked up.

Hanging at the end of a long, long green velvet ribbon that was tied to the second-story chandelier was a clump of mistletoe.

Bev could take a joke, but this was too much, leaving him standing beneath the mistletoe a few days before Christmas. Just thinking about her already had him getting hard. Thank God he had on the stupid coat. He twisted the stud in his ear—a nervous habit.

One of the gnome's eyes looked to be twitching at him. But, no. The light in the hallway was just dim.

Venus—Mrs. Hansen—came down the hall from the kitchen, still walking carefully. Her bright pink yoga pants brushed at her ankles, and her feet were bare. Over the pants she wore one of her long, colorful sweaters, and the neckline came to a deep V. She looked like someone's valentine. V for Venus, V for Valentine. Was she wearing a bra? Her tits were so perfect, Bev suspected that she didn't need to. He began to salivate.

"I hope you like the candy. I made it. There's something for you in the card, too." She held out a bright green gift bag tied closed with pink and white ribbons, and a paper cup with a lid, just like you would get at a coffee shop.

When she met him on the porch steps, he was always a foot or so below her. But now, standing in her hallway, she had to tilt her face up to look in his eyes.

"Mrs...Venus..."

"What is it?" She looked concerned. "Is something wrong?"

Bev dropped the mail onto the table beside the gnome

and turned back to her. His government-issue jacket was bulky, and he wished he'd taken it off but now it was too late. Wrapping his arms around her, he bent his face to hers, focusing on her perfect lips, which were painted the pink of the cotton candy he had always begged for as a child at the state fair—but that his mother would never buy. He breathed deeply of the scents of cinnamon and sugar and the hundred other wonderful smells that surrounded them both before pressing his lips against hers.

She was so tiny in his arms! Who knew a woman could be so delicate? As he moved his lips against hers, hers wouldn't open, but he wouldn't force her because he was a gentleman. Now she was making noise, struggling in his arms and he didn't want to let go because he knew with violent, sudden clarity that it had all been a mistake and maybe if he didn't let her go, then they could pretend it never happened, and...

Unbelievable pain sparked up his gut and into his brain, as she kneed him in the groin.

Venus Hansen was screaming, roaring really, a sound of the kind he'd never heard coming from a woman and definitely not a woman as delicate and pretty as Venus Hansen. He only got a glimpse of her flushed, twisted face as she came at him again because he was doubled over, his brain seared. But he had to protect his head, as well, because she had something hard and wet in her hands and she was striking him with it, again and again and again, and then there was darkness.

Venus touched her swollen lip, getting close to the mirror to get a better look. She couldn't find any other marks on her clothes or body from the postman's attack. He'd finally stopped moving, but she hadn't been able to stop shaking for a good five minutes afterwards. The gnome in her hands had laughed and laughed, then told her that the postman wasn't dead, and that she should finish the job.

Had she been tempted? No. She was certain she was no murderer. It was the postman who had been dangerous!

Should she call the police? What would she tell them?

Hearing the alarm's *beepbeepbeep* that announced a door or window had been opened, she started cautiously down the back stairs. It was too early for the children, and Steffan had surgeries on Thursdays. She didn't see anyone in the back of the house or coming in from the garage. But as she looked down the front hall, she saw the postman was gone from the corner to which he'd retreated and the front door was softly closing.

Tiptoeing to the front door as though the postman still might be able to hear her, Venus peeked out of the sidelight to see him climbing carefully into his truck. He didn't look at the house at all as he turned the truck around and sped down the driveway.

I saved your ass. Now, show me your tits. You owe me.

The gnome lay in a puddle of spilled cider beside the gay little gift bag she'd packed up for the postman. Getting down on one knee—not the injured one—she picked up the gnome. His cheery wooden face looked exactly the same: the pinkish nose, the heavily-lashed eyes, the strange mark that made him seem that he was squinting even though his eyes were perfectly round, exactly alike. But now his beard was splattered with blood.

"Okay, I'll show you. But first let's get you cleaned up." Venus carried the gnome to the kitchen.

The front door beeped and almost immediately slammed again before she heard Mary shouting down the hallway.

"Mommy, Mommy! You didn't come to the bus!"

Mary and Jack burst into the kitchen. In addition to their backpacks and lunch boxes, they bore decorated brown paper bags with "Happy Holidays!" and the name of their school printed on them.

"I got a stupid yo-yo from my secret holiday pal." Mary dumped the contents of her bag on the island. "I think they thought I was a boy. Hey, what's the gnome doing?"

"Eating."

The gnome stood on the breakfast nook table, a bowl of cranberries, walnuts and chocolate chips in front of him.

"Oh, yeah. I guess we forgot to feed him."

"I didn't forget. What did you bring home, honey?" Venus touched Jack's hair as he struggled out of his coat.

"Mini-figs," he said. "I want to wait to open them." He reached into his bag and dug around until he came up with two small bags with Lego figures on them. Then he put them beneath the tree in the family room and came back.

"Are you okay, Mommy? Is your leg still bleeding?" He squatted down and gently patted her knee.

"Mommy is just fine, sweetie." When he stood again, Venus bent to kiss him on the head. She thought of the postman's lips as hers touched Jack's fine blonde hair. Bile rose in her throat and she had to quickly straighten and turn away.

"Did you give the gnome some chocolate chips?" Jack went over to the table and touched the gnome's boots, playing with the rotting leather laces as he always did. "He likes chocolate a lot. He said he would share with me if you gave him some."

Mary scoffed. "He can listen, but can't talk. He's made of wood."

"Maybe he just doesn't talk to you. Maybe he thinks you're a dumbass."

"Mommy!" Mary's outrage came out in a loud whine.

"Jack! What did you say?"

Jack didn't even turn around, but began pushing cranberries and nuts aside in the bowl with his finger. Such a precious, perfect hand. The very first time she'd seen it was on the ultrasound image before he was born, the fingers twitching rhythmically in her fluid-filled womb like some underwater creature waving at her.

"Go to your room and set the timer for ten minutes, Jack Hansen, and when it's done come down and apologize to your sister.

Without looking at either of them, Jack turned and walked casually into the family room and started up the stairs. Venus followed and stood at the bottom, watching him. He'd forgotten to take his shoes off when he first came in the house, and the tread of his tennis shoes had made a path on the carpeted stairs.

"What else did he tell you?" Venus asked, trying to keep her voice light and even. "Did he really talk to you?"

Jack paused on the stair, but didn't turn around. Then he continued up.

"Jack Hansen, I asked you a question."

Still, he mounted the stairs. Silent.

Venus ran up behind him and grabbed his shoulder. "Answer me!"

Unbalanced on the stair, Jack fell backwards onto Venus. She gripped the railing with one hand and wrapped her other arm around him and squeezed. He cried out.

"Tell me what he said. Now."

"You're hurting me!" Jack tried to pull away, but Venus wouldn't let him go.

Venus squeezed his chest harder, and Jack continued to struggle. He coughed, choking, trying to get his breath.

"Mommy, stop!"

Mary was at the bottom of the stairs.

Venus let go of Jack and he stumbled up the rest of the stairs to run to his room. She was breathless. What had she done?

Jack served his penance—more than an hour's worth—and came down to apologize to Mary with what Venus believed was actual sincerity, and Mary had quickly forgiven him. Perhaps, Venus thought, she'd accepted in solidarity with him against her own surprising actions. Yes, she had surprised herself. But she hadn't really hurt him. Jack might pout. One or both of them might even tell Steffan, but she doubted it.

After he apologized to Mary, he came over to Venus and wrapped his arms around her waist and just rested his head against her for a moment. It nearly melted her heart, but he still didn't tell her if the gnome had really spoken to him.

She decided that it could wait.

The children spent a quiet hour and a half after dinner watching *The Polar Express* and making Christmas cards for Venus's parents who would be there Christmas day. Then Mary and Jack went to the kitchen, banishing her to the family room, so they could visit the gnome and make more wishes. Venus had strained to listen, but Jack, who had always been a loud whisperer, had suddenly developed the skill of the quiet whisper.

A thought comforted her: It doesn't matter. He will tell me.

The idea that she was counting on the gnome on the kitchen table to tell her what her children were wishing for unsettled her. It was all so surreal, and Steffan wouldn't even believe her. Nothing felt right. It was as though a shadow had been cast over their happy house and now also lodged inside her, making her feel leaden and sad.

She found Steffan sitting in the leather wing chair in the library, watching a bowl game he'd missed the weekend before. When he'd arrived home, he'd noticed her lip right away, and had seemed satisfied when she told him she'd slipped on the front stairs. As he'd held her she'd begun to relax and almost told him about the postman. But how would she explain it? Had she led the man on in some way? Had she come outside too many times with her workout bra peeking from her sweat jacket? Maybe she'd made him think she was coming on to him.

Now Steffan was relaxed, a bit blurry from his after-dinner Scotch. When he'd kissed her when he first got home, his breath had smelled of mints and wine—inexpensive champagne his office manager, Leslie, had probably picked up for the unofficial holiday party they always had with the gastroenterologist's office that was on the same floor. There was also lipstick on the collar of the blue oxford cloth shirt he wore under the navy cashmere sweater Venus had bought him (she bought all of his clothes), but she hadn't said anything. The worry that he would eventually succumb to one of the pretty women in his office was never far from her mind, and tonight she couldn't let go of the image of Steffan in an illicit embrace with Leslie. Leslie of the nail wraps and long, tan legs. Leslie of the nasty divorce and the deep, luscious voice. Venus clenched her nails to her palm and felt them dig into her skin. But what could she say? Even if she accused him, her own secret about the postman would make her a hypocrite.

She sat on the ottoman, just out of the way of the television.

"Can I ask you something?"

Steffan picked up the remote and muted the game. "What's up, beautiful?" He brushed a bit of hair that had come loose from her ponytail behind her ear. "You look tired. Playing Santa Claus got you down?"

Was he messing with her, pretending to care? She couldn't help but glance at the blot of plum lipstick on the collar, just below his left ear.

"Why did you decide to do the gnome thing for the kids? It…I don't know. It just doesn't seem like you."

He sank back into the chair. "Hey, this gnome thing really bothers you. I thought it would be fun for them. You're always doing things—decorating the house, taking them to pumpkin patches, roller skating." Now he sounded sheepish. "My mother never did that kind of stuff with me, and my dad wasn't around. And I'm…Well, I'm too damn busy to be useful."

"That's all?"

"What do you mean, 'that's all'?"

Venus wasn't quite sure what she meant, only that it had to do with the gnome waiting for her in the kitchen. "Why do you think your mother sent it to us?"

"Honey, why in the hell does my mother do anything? She probably thought we'd put it in the garden. Or in the bathroom. Seriously, I bet she didn't think twice about it."

"I just think it's weird. What if she meant to cause trouble?" It wasn't something Venus had thought of before she said it. In fact, even as Steffan was talking, it had occurred to her that she should find out if the gnome had anything to say about Leslie the office manager.

"Trouble? You're kidding!" Steffan leaned forward. "It's a stupid Christmas Nisse. She likes you, Venus, and she loves the kids. I'm sure she loves you, too."

Venus laughed. "She doesn't even know the kids and hasn't even met Jack. It's not his fault that she won't travel here."

"Yeah, we probably need to go and visit her."

"That's not what I meant." It was an old discussion, one that irritated her. He knew she didn't want to go back there. The horrible memory of the creepy apartment and the awful food and the cigarette smoke hadn't dimmed with time. That a perfectly healthy woman in her early sixties couldn't understand that it was easier for her to travel to their house rather than for the four of them to go to Tromsø, was beyond her.

"Are you asking me not to do the gnome?" Steffan's brow creased. "Because I have something really fun planned for tonight."

* * * * *

Of course he's schtupping the office manager. I can't believe you even asked. I bet he even goes to see her tomorrow.

"That can't be," Venus whispered. "He wouldn't dare."

You're pathetic.

God, was she so pathetic? She'd become a cliché. The betrayed doctor's wife. She told herself that she might have forgiven some drunken one-night stand. But not this.

We need to talk about your kids. They're out of control. That Mary isn't the sharpest knife in the drawer, you know.

There was enough light coming from the family room that she could see the bowl in front of the gnome was empty except for a few walnut crumbs.

"What did they wish for now?"

Jack wants a BB gun so he can shoot you in both eyes.

"Really?" Venus sighed. "What about Mary?"

She wants me to stab the snotty bitch that gave her a stupid yo-yo instead of an iTunes card like the rest of her friends got. And what does the beautiful and clever Venus want?

Was it really possible that her children were wishing for such horrible things? She was beginning to feel as though she didn't know them anymore. Only the gnome seemed terribly familiar. Reliable.

Now she was supposed to wish for something. How odd that it hadn't occurred to her to wish for anything for herself! Weren't wishes for children, and people who spent too much time daydreaming? Perhaps so. She closed her eyes anyway, chewing delicately on her swollen lip, listening to the faint sound of the television coming from down the hallway. Upstairs, her children were sighing in their sleep. She loved them, certainly, despite their changeable natures.

That something in her mind: the nameless shadow trying to take shape. It frightened her, but it was becoming clearer.

Finally, she opened her eyes and bent to whisper in the tiny wooden ear peeking from beneath the gnome's shabby cap.

* * * * *

Venus woke to gray early morning light, thinking it couldn't be later than six a.m. But there were sounds of laughter coming from downstairs, and she rolled onto her side to see that it was already 8:45. Steffan snored undisturbed on the other side of their king bed. Usually she woke up even when the children were trying to be very quiet. It was a mother thing: she was the one on watch, the one who was charged with keeping them safe. But instead of the usual panic she might feel on waking so late, she felt only mild surprise. Her brain was fogged with sleep as though she might still be dreaming, and she had a strong sense that she'd dreamed all through the night, though the dream itself had evaporated with the opening of her eyes.

Leaving Steffan to sleep, she got out of bed to use the bathroom and just pulled on a robe instead of brushing her teeth and putting on workout clothes as she usually did. She felt rested, but still unsettled.

There were only two days left before Christmas.

"Mommy! Mommy! Come see the gnome!"

Mary had raced halfway up the family room stairs to meet her, her diminutive round cheeks flushed, her eyes wide with delight.

"He's so silly! He made it snow in the house!"

The soft blonde leather of the family room's enormous sectional sofa had nearly disappeared in an avalanche of cotton balls. The sections had been pushed together to create a closed rectangle, and not a single cotton ball lay anywhere outside of it. Inside, there were small hillocks like miniature mountains, and on one of these the gnome stood, pitched forward, holding onto two tiny ski poles that looked as though they belonged to one of Mary's dolls. He looked as though he'd been skiing, and had gotten his feet and skis stuck in a drift.

Venus was speechless. The sheer enormity of the display was impressive, even if the effect was terribly strange.

"Can we get in there, Mommy? Please?" Jack, like Mary, was bursting with excitement.

Without waiting for an answer, Mary climbed over one of the sections and landed in the sea of cotton balls. Jack scrambled in after her, squealing.

The cotton balls would soon be everywhere, but Venus didn't feel quite awake enough to object.

"Take a picture of us, Mommy! Where's Daddy? Wait till Daddy sees."

Venus got her phone from the kitchen and came back just in time to see Jack dive for the gnome.

"I can make him ski!"

Mary shouted that he couldn't play with the gnome first because she was the oldest, and Venus was about to tell her to lower her voice when they were both interrupted by a terrified scream from Jack.

Screaming again, Jack threw something against the wall. It wasn't the gnome, which now lay upside down in a valley of cotton fluff. When Venus's eyes tracked back to her son, she covered her mouth lest she also begin screaming.

Mary was silent at first, then gave a loud, nervous laugh.

Jack's hands were covered with blood that dripped onto the snowy field of white, and he kept screaming, screaming, screaming.

"Only the one cut is deep. He got his tetanus booster for day camp this summer, right? He'll be fine." Steffan talked to Venus as though Jack weren't lying right there on their bed, his bandaged hand resting in front of him on the sheet. His eyelids drooped with exhaustion, and his hair, where he'd sweated, was plastered against his forehead. It hadn't been easy for Steffan to get him to take the dose of

Benadryl that would help him rest.

Mary had retreated to the library with a bowl of cereal and permission to watch the Disney Channel for as long as she wanted to that morning.

Venus hadn't spoken once Jack was calm, but as he drifted off to sleep she had to clench her teeth together to keep from yelling at Steffan. She waited until they were in the hallway, their bedroom door half-closed behind them before she turned on him.

"How could you be so careless with a knife? He might have been killed! Were you drunk or something last night?"

Steffan stared. He was still shirtless and in his pajama pants. The scruff of his morning beard glinted in the sunlight. He was heartbroken.

"Jesus, Venus. You think I don't already feel like shit about this? I don't know how it happened."

Venus's voice was low. Furious. "You spent all afternoon drinking with those sluts at the office, and then you were drinking last night. 'Something big,' you told me. This is really goddamn big!"

"What in the hell are you talking about?" The woman in front of him looked ten years older than the Venus he knew: her eyes seemed to have sunken further into her head, and her cheeks were hollow. She had perhaps even lost weight. He wasn't sure what had happened to her in the past few days, but something was changing her. And now she was so angry, he thought she might strike him. Maybe he deserved some kind of punishment. But he knew it had been an accident. He must have put the open pocketknife down as he placed the gnome, and it sank into the cotton balls.

"You know exactly what I'm talking about." Venus pushed at his chest. "You show up here half-drunk after screwing around all afternoon, and expect me not to care. And then you nearly kill one of your kids."

"Venus." Now Steffan was worried. She really wasn't

herself. He tried to put a hand on her shoulder, but she pushed him away.

"Just stop. Just get away."

"You're acting insane. It was an accident, and you damn well know it!" Steffan pushed past her. His footfalls thundered down the back stairs.

Venus followed, and saw him stop by the nest of cotton balls, now spotted with blood. He picked up the pocketknife from the floor, where it had landed when Jack had thrown it. Even from the stairs she could see the blade, dull with her child's blood.

It no longer felt like Christmastime. Jack woke up hungry, and Steffan carried him downstairs where Venus helped him eat blueberry pancakes and hot chocolate. He resisted her help at first, saying that he wasn't a baby, but the bandage made his right hand awkward, and Venus promised that she would only have to help him for a day or two.

Mary patted Jack's shoulder, telling him that she was sure the gnome didn't mean for him to get hurt. Jack's eyes looked to the gnome, who was now on the kitchen desk, his cheery face looking just as it had when he'd first come out of the box.

"I know," Jack whispered.

Venus and Steffan were supposed to go to a caroling party at the home of one of the founding doctors in the practice, a man who preferred the humble pleasures of his twenty-room house in the historic district to the skiing holidays of his fellow practitioners. But Venus called the doctor's wife, pleading that one of the children was sick, and then canceled the sitter. She didn't bother to tell Steffan. If he called independently or even went on his own, that was his problem. She hadn't spoken to him all day. He'd cleaned up the cotton balls, stuffing them into big green yard bags, and set the furniture back where it belonged. Then he left the house without telling anyone where he was going.

Steffan pulled out of the driveway, energized by the cold. He'd been desperate to get out of the house. The heat was turned up way above normal, and he had no idea why. But he wasn't about to ask.

What in the hell was happening? He drove to get a latte, then sat in the parking lot watching the cars packed with last-minute shoppers go in and out of the shopping mall across the street. His present for Venus was in the glovebox of the car, already wrapped. He tried to imagine her opening the diamond bracelet he'd chosen so carefully last week, but couldn't see it in his head. Just a few days earlier, everything had been so good.

Now his wife was acting insane, and he didn't feel so sane himself. He'd been sleeping badly, and, yes, he might have had too much to drink the previous day. Maybe he did need to ease off on the booze. But he hadn't screwed around at work. That was all in Venus's head.

The gnome game had been fun. God, he'd tried. All the elf tricks he'd found on the Internet had seemed so dumb. He wanted to be the clever dad. The original dad. The *best* dad.

He sat watching the cars until his coffee was gone. Then he backed out of the space and headed into the crush of the shoppers. At least he could buy Jack and Mary some small surprises from their dad—even if they thought they were from the gnome. *Combat pay.*

As he entered the mall, his cell phone rang. He didn't recognize the number, but, worried that it might be about Jack, he answered.

The voice on the other end of the line sounded close, so much closer than it had in a very long time. "Steffan, my dear Steffan. I'm here. I'm here to surprise you!"

When he saw her enter the baggage claim at the airport, he didn't recognize her as his mother at first. She had shrunk in the six years since he'd seen her, and her red and gold hair had dulled and lay flat against her head. This woman looked uncertain, her eyes faded, her hands fumbling anxiously at the strap of her handbag. But he immediately recognized the coat: a sturdy gray wool, knee-length dress coat of the sort she'd worn since he was a boy. Where she was able to buy them, decade after decade, he had no idea.

As they drove up to the house, set so far back from the road, she gasped at the loveliness of the scene. The moon was out, and the Christmas lights covering the bushes and outlining the porch and roof twinkled against the night. Steffan was overwhelmed with a feeling of pride that his mother would finally see what he'd done, what his life had become. How he'd made something of her sacrifices.

And he was a little stunned that his wish had come true.

"You planned this with her, didn't you?" was all Venus said when they were alone in their bedroom.

The children were in bed, but Venus had still been awake when Steffan and his mother arrived. She was surprised to see Helen, but even in her unusual state quickly recovered her manners, falling into the role of hostess—a role she was very good at. They all agreed that they wouldn't wake the children, but would wait for introductions in the morning.

Steffan stood in the bathroom doorway, toothbrush in

hand. "That's crazy. You know me better than that."

Venus pulled the covers up around her ears and turned her back on him.

"Venus, she told us both that she said she didn't plan to come. You heard her. She got some sort of Christmas bonus and thought it would be a nice surprise for the kids. It's the one spontaneous thing she's done in her life. I thought you'd be glad."

There was only silence from the bed.

Too tired to try to engage her, Steffan went downstairs and started to pour himself a bourbon. But he changed his mind and made cocoa instead. After a few brief words to the silent gnome, whose cheery face looked only slightly sinister in the dim light coming from the family room, Steffan set up one final pre-Christmas tableau. Screw Venus if she didn't like it.

Steffan was mistaken. Venus knew he thought she was angry that Helen had arrived, unannounced. But her coming *had* been announced. The gnome had told her the day before, soon after Steffan left the house.

She's coming.

"Who is coming?"

His mother is coming. He wished it. He wished it so they could kill you, and have her here to take care of the children. He thinks you're not fit to raise them.

The words hurt, but Venus knew the gnome was telling the truth. But she couldn't let Steffan know that she knew. She would watch him, and wait as long as she needed to.

"Mary, Jack, this is Grandma Helen." Steffan had his arm firmly around his mother's frail shoulders as though she might wander off, or needed protection.

The children watched their grandmother shyly, Jack reaching his bandaged hand along the breakfast nook table to Mary for reassurance.

"Oh, you poor Jack. What happened to your hand?" Helen asked.

Steffan watched Jack glance at the kitchen island where the gnome stood in one of Jack's plastic toy boats, tiny wrapped packages at his feet, surrounded by a colorful ocean whose waves were made of Venus's stained glass candy. Steffan had been careful not to cover the gnome's feet as he had the previous day with the cotton balls. There was nothing hidden.

"It was an accident," Mary said, her voice barely a whisper.

"Let's get you some coffee and breakfast, Helen. You must be starving." Venus filled up the water reservoir on the single-cup coffee maker. "You're hours ahead of us—it's almost dinnertime for you."

Every word that Venus said to the woman hurt coming out of her mouth. The enemy was under her roof. The gnome had told her she was coming, but she hadn't quite believed it. She should've known better.

Now Helen pointed to the gnome. "Tell me about this. I've never seen such a thing."

Steffan and Venus both stared at her. Steffan held his breath, thinking at lightning speed, wondering how the thing had gotten here if his mother hadn't sent it. What it might mean. Suddenly the gnome's sinister look seemed more significant, and everything Steffan understood about how the world worked was in question.

Venus broke the spell. "But you sent it."

Helen laughed. "Yes, I did. But I never thought I'd see it in a boat, with candy around it. How very clever."

Venus decided to push her. "So I guess he was one of your gnomes? I know you have so many."

"Oh, no. I found him at a shop a friend of mine owns. He seemed very special. I translated the poem because I thought the children would like it." She beamed at Mary with her yellowed teeth and bare, brownish lips.

Steffan was relieved at his mother's explanation, but he didn't like the nasty, sarcastic edge in Venus's voice. She'd put on lipstick and yoga pants with a sweater the color of a pistachio nut, but she hadn't brushed her hair. He wondered at her carelessness. As with so many things these days, it wasn't like her.

"Did you set up this scene with the boat, Venus? So creative," Helen said.

Mary spoke up. "The Christmas Gnome does it. He says it's mischief. I read it in the poem."

"You can read? How wonderful, Mary. You must read me something while I'm here."

An awkward discussion followed when Mary asked where her other grandparents would sleep when they arrived the next day. Christmas Day.

"We'll sort it out," Venus finally said, grinning. "It will be just fine."

It was a beautiful Christmas Eve. Before the sun set, Venus called the children out to the porch to see that snow had begun to fall—not a lot, but enough that the grass sparkled with a thin layer of white crystal. A dozen late-feeding cardinals the color of holly berries silently flitted between the bushes, the ground and the feeder.

She'd made the only decision she could, and she was at peace with it. The gnome had mocked her, told her she'd never get away with it, but she knew she had to try. Helen was here to replace her. There was no other reason for her to come. She'd sent the gnome ahead to frighten her, to make her hurt the people she loved. But it was Helen who wouldn't get away with it.

"Is that the Christmas Star?" Jack pointed to the sky's single star that seemed to float between the dramatic purple clouds only a few inches from the nearly transparent moon.

"No," Mary said. "It's a planet."

"I think it's Venus." Steffan had come out to stand behind them and put a tentative hand on Venus's shoulder. She didn't move. Didn't dare let herself feel too much, or trust him too much.

Watch him, the gnome had said.

They stood, silent, until another large cloud covered both the moon and the planet, and Mary complained that she was cold. Steffan's hand fell away from Venus's shoulder. It was the last time he would touch her.

Inside, she prepared a simple supper of leftover chili for Steffan, Helen and herself, and macaroni and cheese for the children, who could barely eat for the excitement of its being Christmas Eve. After Steffan had changed the bandages on Jack's right hand he was better able to hold a fork. Helen watched him eat, but didn't ask any more questions. They all laughed at her story about Steffan's first time seeing snow when he was a boy in northern Georgia, how they had tried to build a snowman, but it had ended up being mostly grass and mud. After dinner, Steffan brought in his laptop so Jack and Mary could track Santa and his sleigh on NORAD while they watched *The Polar Express* for the 10th time that season.

Venus watched her. Watched Steffan.

When she went into the kitchen alone, the gnome whispered to her.

Ho. Ho. Ho. Tonight's the big night. This I've got to see.

After Helen closed the door to the guest room, Steffan and Venus put both children to bed in the twin beds in Mary's room. Steffan sat on the edge of Mary's bed. Venus knelt beside Jack.

"How can I open presents?" Jack held his bandaged

hand up. His face was serious, his eyes studying Venus.

"Jesus's birthday is the best present. But I don't think you're going to have any problem, Jack-o."

"You never call me Jack-o anymore, Mommy. That's when I was a baby."

Venus brushed his bangs aside and kissed his forehead, letting her lips linger on his warm skin.

"I love you, Jack-o."

Outside Mary's room, Steffan stopped her before she went downstairs.

"Do you need help with the presents? I'd like to help."

"No." Venus couldn't read his eyes in the hall's half-light, but then she didn't really want to. "I'll do it alone." She left him standing in the hallway.

Venus hummed a Christmas carol. *Here comes Santa Claus.* The presents were under the tree. Everything needed to be *just so.*

Hey hey ho, hey hey ho. Off to work, eh, girlie?

"Shhhhhh."

No worries. They can't hear. Baby, it's cold outside. Where's your coat?

He was right. It *was* cold outside. Venus got her warmest coat from the closet, and put it on. She pulled on her snow boots, as well. The snow wasn't deep—maybe two inches, but it might get worse. She carried the gnome upside down, by his feet.

Let's go.

Venus took the back stairs as quietly as she could. Stopping by the master bedroom door, she put her ear to it, touched it lightly with her fingertips. Nothing. She passed by the children's rooms and opened the guest room door.

The white glow coming from the Christmas lights outside the window illuminated the bedroom enough that

Venus could see Helen lying in the bed. An odor of cigarette smoke came from the bathroom even though Venus had asked her not to smoke in the house. Cigarettes and a lighter sat on the bedside table.

If you don't do it to her, it will be you who will die.

"Helen."

The woman on the bed didn't stir.

"Helen."

Helen opened her eyes. She looked confused a moment, then said, "What do you want?"

Venus squatted near the bed, letting the gnome's head in its sorry hat rest on the floor. "I want to know why you're here."

Pushing the blanket away from her emaciated body, Helen sighed.

Her chest was concave beneath the cotton camisole she wore, and her slight breasts sagged inward as well. Even in the poor light, Venus could see how spotted with age her skin was.

"To see," she said. "I wanted to see what would happen to you."

The gnome chuckled.

"Can you hear him?" Venus said. "I can hear him."

"I don't need to hear him."

Venus listened to the sounds of her sleeping house. Sounds she knew she would never hear again.

Helen sat up and reached for her cigarettes and matches. Venus watched, mesmerized, as Helen took out one of the cigarettes and lighted it. She exhaled the smoke so that it hung like fog in the mellow glow of the Christmas lights.

"You're rude," Helen finally said. "And you're weak. It's too bad you didn't succeed in killing yourself before you met Steffan. All your smug, prissy notes, and whiny phone calls. Practically begging me to give a damn about you. You're wired so tightly, someday you were going to snap, anyway."

"Why didn't you just stay away?" Venus felt like she wanted to cry, but she didn't want to give Helen the satisfaction.

Helen leaned toward her. "He's in your head, isn't he? He's in your head and he's not going to go away, Venus. He's there forever. He'll be there when they take you away. He'll be there until you die." She took another drag from the cigarette. "There's nothing you can do."

"Now I know," Venus said, standing.

Do it! Do it! Dooooooooo it!

Venus caught Helen beneath her right jaw, first, then hit her on the side of the head, again and again, forcing her back onto the bed. She was so quick, Helen didn't have time to scream before she stopped moving. Venus had learned her lesson with the postman and finished the job even without the gnome's instruction.

Helen's burning cigarette had landed on the blanket, which had begun to smolder. Venus let it lie there.

Before leaving the room, Venus went to the window and held the gnome up to see if he'd been stained.

"Stop laughing," she whispered.

It's just so funny. I can't help myself.

Tired of his voice, Venus picked up a wool scarf that Helen had left on a chair and wound it around him.

I'm still here.

How odd that the gnome's voice wasn't muffled at all, as though he were whispering right into her ear.

Burn, baby, burn.

Helen's hair and camisole had caught fire, and the flames overlaid the bed like a second, brilliant blanket.

Venus left the bedroom, quietly closing the door behind her.

Down in the kitchen, she grabbed a handful of the stained glass candy she'd labored over—and, no, she hadn't missed the fact that Steffan had wasted half of it on his boat display—and shoved it into her coat pocket. The front door gave its three quick *beeps* as she opened it and went outside.

The snow was falling in earnest, and the moon had disappeared. She headed toward the woods with only the Christmas lights to guide her across the spotless, white lawn. The sky above her quickly disappeared into the tops of the trees, and she heard nothing else—not the frantic bleating of the smoke alarms inside the house, nor Steffan's shouts for her and the children. All was silence, until the gnome finally spoke.

He'll get them out, you know. He'll always keep them safe. You'll get your wish.

"I know."

THE CHRISTMAS SPIRIT

by

LISA MORTON

"MERRY CHRISTMAS, SWEETHEART."

Ray handed her a small package wrapped simply in tissue paper with a length of hemp cord wound around it.

Elise looked up in surprise; the clock on the mantel read just after four. "Why so early?" She regretted the words as soon as she said them; she knew Ray would think she was refusing the gift. She tried to recover with a smile as she reached for the present.

He handed it over. "Just open it."

She did, with an odd knot of dread in her stomach. Things hadn't been good between them for a while, ever since the fertility experts had been unable to help them conceive. Elise had inherited Great Aunt Priscilla's house a month ago, and they'd decided to get out of the city, leave London and spend the holiday at the old country place before they put it on the market. It was an isolated cottage,

71

situated near a peat bog in the Yorkshire countryside. Aunt Priscilla hadn't actually lived in it for years, having forsaken the isolation for the relative comforts of the city. It'd taken them six hours to negotiate the holiday traffic coming up from London, and the place was a slight let-down – neither old enough to be romantic and intriguing, nor nice enough to bring a decent price. "Dear God," Ray had said as he'd pulled their bags from the car, his feet crunching on ice and gravel, "someone actually lived out here?"

The inside was dusty and dim, with just enough furniture left behind to make it function as a residence. Elise had brought a few Christmas decorations along, but the strings of twinkling lights and fragrant green wreaths did little to enliven the gloom.

That arrival had been two days ago. They'd quarreled and retreated to silence since; today, the 24th, Ray had spent most of the day in the village while Elise had puttered in the kitchen with a roast and Christmas pudding. Now she tried to act happy as she unwrapped the gift, but she was imagining it as something sarcastic and cruel – a baby name book, perhaps.

It *was* a book, an old hardback bound in plain green cloth. She opened it and read the title page:

The Christmas Spirit
by
Mrs. H. Warren
Privately Printed by the Author
1895

"I FOUND IT IN THE ANTIQUE STORE IN the village," Ray said. "The proprietor thought the author might have lived around here."

Elise flipped forward a few pages, looking for a clue about why Ray had bought this, but she found only a first chapter about a young widow spending Christmas with an eccentric aunt. She looked up at Ray, trying to seem merely curious.

"Remember last week, we were talking about how people once read ghost stories to each other on Christmas Eve? I thought maybe we could read this aloud tonight. Might be fun."

"Oh, yes – of course." Elise closed the book and saw the author's name in gilt on the spine – Mrs. H. Warren. There was something vaguely familiar about the name, but she couldn't place it. "I wonder who she was, and why she had this privately printed…"

Ray laughed as he headed for the kitchen, going for the wine. "She probably wasn't good enough to sell to a real publisher. Nowadays she'd just put her self-published e-book online."

"Probably."

By the time Ray came back with a glass of Merlot, Elise had read the first two pages. "Actually, it's not bad."

He sipped the red wine, settled into the worn old green couch before the hearth, and said, "Read it to me."

"Now? Shouldn't we do it after dinner, when it's dark?"

Ray shrugged. After eight years of marriage, Elise knew that gesture meant he wasn't happy, but he didn't think it was worth fighting over. She relented. "Tell you what: Pour me a glass of that, and I'll start reading."

Smiling, Ray rose, heading to the kitchen.

The smell of the roasting meat filled the house, a small fire glowed from the hearth, and Elise tried to feel comfortable in the house, but she couldn't. She remembered visiting it once as a child. That had been in June, but even then the house had been chilly, and there was something Elise could only describe as "oppressive" about its atmosphere. Her Great Aunt Priscilla had lived here then, surrounded by frilly pieces of the past – ceramic dog figures, tatted doilies, ruffled pillows, framed photographs of other people's children – but Elise wondered if all the manufactured cheeriness had been her aunt's attempt at covering up the essential gloom of the house.

There'd been something else on that visit, something Elise had never confessed to her skeptical husband: She'd been playing outside, alone, in a small out-building that served as a combination storage shed/garage. She'd felt an odd sensation, like a chill without a cold temperature, and had turned to see a man watching her. He was inside the garage, in the farthest, darkest corner. Even shadowed as he was, she saw quite plainly his old-fashioned suit, his handsome face, his large hands. "Hello," she said.

He didn't answer.

"Do you know my aunt?"

He continued to stare.

Eight-year-old Elise felt another chill, and turned to race back to the house. She bounded into the kitchen, where her mother and aunt were preparing tea. "Aunty Priscilla, who's that man in the garage?"

"What man, dear?"

"He wouldn't tell me his name, but he's wearing very old clothes, like something from a black and white movie."

Priscilla, already a pale, older woman, had gone completely white. Elise's mum had noticed, grabbing at Priscilla's arm in concern. "Are you all right? What is it?"

"Oh, it's…" Priscilla shook her head before continuing, "…there's no one there, dear. Just a pile of old cans with some towels draped over them. You're not the first one to see something there."

"But I *did* see a man." Elise turned to her mother. "Mummy, there *is* a man out there, come see –"

Mum had cast a quick look at Priscilla, whose expression remained carefully blank. "I'll be right back."

Priscilla just nodded.

Elise led her mother across the yard to the outbuilding. She raised her hand to point. "He's back –"

She broke off as she realized they were alone. No man in an antiquated suit; just what Priscilla had described, a stack of containers and cleaning cloths.

"There, darling, you see? Aunty Priscilla was right. There's no one there."

Elise hadn't openly protested, but she knew what she'd seen. A man.

Or…something that was not a man.

That'd been nearly thirty years ago. Not long after that, Priscilla had moved and the house had been forgotten, until a few weeks ago when Elise had been shocked to find that Priscilla had died with no other kin and had left her estate to her grand-niece. There wasn't much – a small bank account, some old belongings, a family album that Elise found fascinating – and Elise doubted the old cottage would be worth much. Unless it could save her marriage.

She heard footsteps overhead, and wondered why Ray had gone upstairs. Perhaps he'd forgotten something –

Ray returned from the kitchen, extending a full glass to her. She took it, puzzled. "Were you just upstairs?"

"No. Why?"

"Odd. I heard footsteps."

Ray set the rest of the wine bottle on the table near the couch and resumed his seat there. "Ooh, that sounds like the beginning of the ghost story right there."

"Hardly." Elise sipped her wine, then picked up Mrs. Warren's book. "This was written in 1895, so don't expect CGI effects."

"Just read."

Elise cleared her throat and began. "Chapter One…"

The Christmas Spirit
by
Mrs. H. Warren

Chapter One

AT TWENTY-THREE, I WAS TOO YOUNG TO be a widow, or at least that's what everyone told me.

But accidents don't care who's too young or too old;

75

they're impartial when it comes to age. Otherwise, my Henry would still be alive, instead of moldering in a grave at the age of twenty-four.

"A freak accident", they called it. No one could have foreseen the machinery blowing apart in quite so spectacular a fashion at the exact instant that the factory foreman – Henry – was walking past. A plate-sized cog wheel caught him in the head. They said the machinery could never have been expected to do that, that it was really quite safe. They told me it had been instantaneous, that he hadn't suffered.

I, on the other hand, certainly had.

Henry and I had been married for two years. At the time we were wed, I had no family to speak of except dear old Aunt Vanessa; Henry, on the other hand, had family, but despised them all and invited none of them to the wedding. Until we could start our own family, we were really all each other had.

But we hadn't been blessed with children yet. We'd bought a lovely little place just outside Manchester; it had enough room for the son and daughter we hoped for. We clung to the notion that my own mother had had me late in her life – she'd been in her thirties – so perhaps ours would simply arrive later.

Then my world was taken from me. Henry was dead. There would be no children.

He'd left me with enough money to survive on for the immediate future, but when he died it was two weeks before Christmas, and I was quite naturally devastated, to the point where Aunt Vanessa feared I might attempt something foolish. She wrote me letters daily, urging me to join her for Christmas. "Dearest Jane," the letters would say, "you know how I care for you and worry about your future, because you're really all I have left." She even suggested that I might consider a permanent move.

I wasn't ready yet to give up our little Manchester home, but the idea of spending Christmas alone also held no appeal to me, so on the 21ˢᵗ of December I wrote her back to tell her I was coming. It took me a day to make arrangements, and I was off.

The train north was decent, but finding transportation from the station to Aunty's cottage proved more difficult – Carlton Abbey, the village where I disembarked, had no regular cab service. I finally found a man who agreed to drive me out in his open hay wagon, but because it was now late in the day, we'd have to wait until tomorrow morning.

"Nobody goes out that way towards dark," he muttered, in the thick local accent.

Luckily the village inn had a room to let; it was clean and quite tolerable. The bartender's wife was a kindly middle-aged woman named Sarah who had broad hips and vivid red cheeks. She brought me a bowl of savory stew once my bags had been taken upstairs and surprised me by asking if she could sit with me and talk for a few minutes. "Of course," I answered.

She pulled out one of the sturdy pub chairs and addressed me with a serious tone. "I don't mean to pry, miss, but…how much do you know about that old house and your aunt?"

The question surprised me. "Not much about the house, and only a little more about Aunt Vanessa."

"Have you visited these parts before?"

I shook my head. "No. I've only met my aunt a few times, and those were always when she visited my family. We never came to see her."

Sarah thought for a moment, and then said, "The house is not right."

"Whatever do you mean? Is it unsafe?"

"In a manner of speaking. And your aunt – she's not a bad sort, but there are things about her you don't know."

"Such as…?"

Sarah caught her husband watching her from behind the bar as he polished glasses with a towel. She lowered her eyes, pulling away from the table. "It's not my place to say more. Just...be cautious, miss."

She left, returning to the kitchen. After a few moments her husband followed, and I heard a muffled conversation occur between them.

I finished the excellent stew and returned to my upstairs room without seeing them again. The bed was comfortable enough, the fireplace kept the temperature at an adequate level, but sleep eluded me. I kept going over Sarah's words in my head. Something was wrong with the house? And my aunt apparently possessed – what, disturbing qualities she'd kept hidden from the rest of her family?

I would find out the answers to these questions soon enough.

Elise lowered the book. "And that's the end of Chapter One."

Smirking, Ray said, "I think I've seen this movie before. It's not exactly wildly original, is it?"

"It does feel a bit like a Hammer horror movie. Still, I like its earnest tone. Shall I keep going?"

Ray poured himself another glass of wine, and Elise realized he was already drunk. "Why not? Let's hear all about Aunty."

Elise returned to the book. "Chapter Two..."

The next morning – the 23rd – dawned chilly and gray. Outside, snow was falling; it had already piled up against the sides of Carlton Abbey's few buildings. I wondered if my trip to the house would be delayed, but Mr. Murphy, the wagon driver, appeared at the inn at exactly 8 a.m. He handed me a rough woolen blanket. "Here, miss – you'll need that for the trip."

We loaded my bags onto his buckboard wagon. The two horses drawing the contraption stamped in the cold, their breath coming in cloudy snorts. Finally we took our places on the open driver's bench, tugging hats and cuffs and blankets into place. Mr. Murphy gave the reins a little flip, and off we went.

It's possible that, at some point in my life, I've been colder, but if so I have no memory of it. I wondered if we wouldn't have been better off in a sleigh, but the snow hadn't built up much yet and the simple but tough wagon served fine. Mr. Murphy wasn't a loquacious companion, but I did learn that he made this trip once a week, bringing food and supplies to my aunt. Occasionally he brought her into the village so she could tend to various matters, but I was the first visitor he'd brought out to her.

The trip took about an hour. By the time we passed the peat bog and the cottage appeared behind a whitened hedge, I wondered if I might have frostbite. I was moving stiffly as I stepped down from the wagon and heard a voice from the house: "Oh my dear, my Jane, come inside at once!"

I hadn't seen my Aunt in twenty years, and my memories of her were colored by childhood's perceptions. I remembered her as a small, neat, very pretty woman with a sweeping mass of dark hair. Now she was mostly silver-haired, prematurely bent and slightly pudgy. The lines of her face were still clear and striking, though, and she moved easily, without the stiffness I was currently conveying. She rushed out, took my arm, and led me into the cottage. Mr. Murphy followed behind with my bags.

Aunt Vanessa took me into her parlour and gave me the seat of honor closest to the fireplace, which currently blazing. I let her remove the heavy blanket and my outer wraps, and hand me a cup of steaming tea. Seeing me settled, she went outside again with Murphy. They returned a few moments later with several boxes of supplies. Mr. Murphy hastily gulped a cup down, accepted payment, doffed his hat once, and then turned to go. "Merry Christmas to you and your family, Mr. Murphy," she called after him.

When he was gone she closed the door behind him before joining me in the parlour. "Now, darling Jane, tell me how you are."

"Thawing," I said, my teeth still chattering.

We chatted amiably for a bit, about the dreadful weather, and my train trip, and the world outside Carlton Abbey. Finally I seemed to have reached room temperature, and Aunt Vanessa showed me to my room. Mr. Murphy had already carried my bags there.

It was charming, with a large, fluffy bed, a small fireplace, dresser, basin, mirror, rocker, window seat. The decorations were warm and comforting. Aunt Vanessa suggested I take a rest before supper, and I agreed. I'd slept little at the inn; now that I was here and warm again, I was surprisingly drowsy. I lay down on the bed, thinking merely to test it, and drifted off almost instantly.

I awoke when someone came into the room.

I was half-asleep when I heard the footsteps. Thinking it was my aunt peeking in to check on me, I opted for a few more minutes of sleep and didn't open my eyes. But then I had the sensation of someone standing over me, and so I did force myself awake. I looked up to see that the light in the room had dimmed – the fire had gone out, the light spilling in through the window was less – and it took a few seconds for me to make out anything. Then I saw: A silhouetted figure at the foot of the bed. A large figure, with broad shoulders. A man, in other words.

I tried to call out, but couldn't seem to move, to even force sounds from my throat. My limbs were equally unresponsive, my heart hammered but uselessly. I was paralyzed.

He stood there for some time, not moving, not speaking. I couldn't make out his face or any particulars about him.

I finally closed my eyes, tightly, as if I could somehow make him vanish by refusing to see him. Almost immediately, I felt something in the room change – it lightened again, a crushing sense of essential *wrongness* gone. I opened my eyes.

He was gone.

I took a few moments to collect myself – to let my heartbeat return to its usual pace – before I rose and left the room behind. I found my aunt in the kitchen, sipping tea and writing in a journal which she closed as I entered. "Ah, there you are. Did you nap well, dear?"

"Aunt Vanessa, who is the man I saw in my room?"

Her polite smile disappeared instantly, her shoulders slumped, she set the teacup down, rattling it in the saucer. "Oh. Oh dear. I'd hoped this wouldn't happen…"

"That what wouldn't happen?" I sat down across from her and poured myself a cup of tea from the pot in the center of the table.

"That you wouldn't meet Joe."

"Who's Joe?"

"Our ghost, dear."

I set the cup down and stared at her, incredulous. "Ghost? But surely…"

"Oh, please, dear Jane, don't tell me there are no such things, or that you don't believe in them." She stood, pumped more water into the tea kettle, and hung it over the kitchen fire.

"Aunty, do you mean to say that you think your house is *haunted*?"

She returned, sat across from me, and fixed me with a resolute stare. "I don't 'think' it, dear – I *know* it. Joe, you see, is a man named Joseph Hood, and he died here under rather tragic circumstances thirty-six years ago." She broke off as her eyes took on a distant look, then she continued. "In fact it will be exactly thirty-six years ago tomorrow."

"He died on Christmas Eve?"

Aunt Vanessa nodded. "He was intoxicated. He came into the living room, dropped something near the hearth, tried to reach for it but tripped and fell into the fire."

I realized she was referring to the same hearth I'd warmed myself before just a short time earlier, and I shuddered. "How horrible."

"They said he at least didn't suffer – he knocked himself out when he fell."

"Who was he? Did you know him?"

My aunt looked away, and I had the distinct sense that she was covering something up, or being less than completely forthcoming. "Yes. He...worked for me. Just a local fellow. I was the one who found him, in fact."

The way she choked up on the last bit seemed authentic, and I had a rush of sympathy for her. I stood and moved behind her so I could rest my hands on her shoulders in an empathetic way. "Oh, Aunt Vanessa, I'm so sorry."

She reached up and patted my hands with hers. "It's really quite all right, dear – it was such a long time ago. And frankly, having Joe around since has frequently been...well, interesting."

I resumed my seat and decided to humor her. "What does he do?"

"Oh, he's quite harmless. He might slam a cabinet door, or knock on a wall. He must be quite impressed with you – I don't actually see him all that often."

After that, we talked about other things. I told Vanessa about my life with Henry, and she told me about her family growing up. They were an intriguing group of people, this part of my family I didn't know at all – a collection of eccentrics that included a tea trader who'd sold opium in China, a madwoman who'd died in an asylum, and a professional street mummer.

We chattered away through the late afternoon, past sunset, and well into the night. Finally Aunt Vanessa yawned and said she needed to seek the solace of her bed.

I was initially uncomfortable with the thought of returning to my room, but I soon convinced myself that whatever trick of light and shadow I'd seen couldn't possibly exist at night, and so I retired as well, taking a book with me. I stoked the little fire and slid under the blankets, convinced that sleep would elude me…but after an hour of wading through the sadly-dull book, my eyes became heavy and I slid into a deep and dreamless slumber.

Elise lowered the book and looked around the house. Ray poured more wine for both of them. "Was that the end of the chapter?"

"Yes," Elise said, distractedly. After a few seconds, she added, "You know what's odd? The house in this book could be the very one we're in."

Ray followed her gaze around the room. "True, but I would imagine that most of the old country houses were built like this."

"I suppose so…still…"

Ray smiled. "It's more fun to believe it's the *same* house, is that it?"

"You caught me."

He laughed and toasted her. "Please continue. This is so much more entertaining than watching another Fanny Cradock re-run on the telly."

Elise – who loved cooking shows – shot her husband a vicious look before raising the book again. "Chapter Three…"

I awoke in the morning surprisingly refreshed and happy to be where I was. Yesterday's storm had passed, and the day was bright, with just the occasional puffy white cloud scudding past the sun.

Aunt Vanessa and I spent the day like two old sisters, nattering about in the kitchen preparing foods for a Christmas dinner that could have fed ten. We fixed goose and mincemeat and puddings and popcorn; we even made a wassail bowl, although there were only two of us and we had no intentions of going wassailing come evening. The lovely scent of the wassail – cider, cinnamon, nutmeg – mixed with the other food smells to fill the house with a cheerful holiday scent.

Day passed into evening. We laid out our merry feast and indulged ourselves. We were soon both quite besotted from the wassail. I'd never been much for drink; even a small amount went straight to my head. By midnight we were both reeling and stumbling as we wished each other a Merry Christmas and made our way to our rooms.

I undressed and crawled beneath the covers, warm from the drink and the food and the pleasant evening. The little fire began to die down as I headed into sleep.

At some point in the night I became aware of a dream I was having. I was still disoriented from the wassail, and unsure where I was. I felt another in bed beside me, felt the firm muscles of a man, and thought I must be dreaming of Henry. It would only be later on that I would realize how odd it was – if not close to impossible – to be so self-aware during a dream that you *knew* you were dreaming.

I shan't describe the dream in detail here, for it progressed in an extremely intimate fashion. Suffice to say I was ecstatic to give myself over to it, to have my Henry for one more evening. Even though he was somewhat rougher, more impassioned, than I recalled him having ever been, I considered this dream of Henry to be the most cherished Christmas gift imaginable.

A terrible headache awoke me in the morning, the after-effects of my wassail consumption. For a few seconds, I felt only the grinding pain in my temples, ears, and just above my teeth. Then I realized I was unclothed beneath the blankets, although I'd gone to bed in my usual proper nightgown, which lay discarded on the floor beside the bed. Increasingly alarmed, I drew back the covers, and saw small red splotches dotting the white linen. I looked down at myself, and saw the blood had come from crescent-shaped marks on my shoulders and bosom. They were unquestionably bite marks, and their pain was a large part of my headache.

I bit back a scream and leapt from the bed. That was when I saw it – red marks dabbed on the pillow that had just been beneath my head, marks that formed seven letters. The letters read:

LOVE JOE

I did cry out then, not so much a scream as a sort of prolonged sob. It was enough to rouse my aunt, who proceeded to bang against my door, calling my name. She asked me why I'd locked the door, and I realized I *hadn't*. I went to it and turned the lock, and she entered.

When she saw me, she gasped loudly. She was asking what happened when she saw the bed – or, more specifically, the pillow.

Her expression went cold, and she said, "You need to leave here. Today. NOW."

I didn't argue. I requested only the time it would take for me to attend to my wounds and gather my things.

She waited for me in the living room. When I came in, struggling with my bags, she told me to leave them, that she'd have them sent later. She had a neighbor less than a quarter-mile distant who had a horse and carriage; he could take me back to the village.

She offered no kind word of sympathy, no apology or explanation. Nor did I ask for any.

Together, we walked out into the chilly Christmas morn. It was overcast again, though not snowing yet. Our breath came out in opaque puffs as we trudged along the lane. We finally reached her neighbors, the Lees. They were a family of five, simple farmers with generous dispositions, who rushed to my side in concern when Aunty told them I'd fallen ill and needed immediate transportation to the village. They agreed instantly; the father, George, went out to hitch the horses to their carriage.

Aunt Vanessa gave me a rather cool embrace, muttered something about being sorry our Christmas had ended so poorly, and then left.

Once she was gone, I asked George's wife Annie who Joe Hood was. She gaped for a second, and then bade me sit down as she made a hot cup of tea for me. She sat beside me as I sipped the good, strong tea, and she told me the story of Joe.

"You may believe your aunt to be a lifelong spinster, but the truth of the matter is that she was married once – to Joe Hood. She was twenty, and although you might not know it now, she was considered a beauty among the local folk. She wasn't rich, but she'd been left enough money to live comfortably for the rest of her life.

"Because of all that she had any number of suitors, but only one caught her fancy: Joseph Hood was a young man who'd come up from the south – some said he'd been run off after a scandal with a society lady – and he was very comely. He saw an easy life with your aunt, so he wooed her. They were married just three months after they met, and Joe moved into the cottage with your aunt.

"That's when she found out what kind of man Joe Hood really was: He drank, he cursed if asked to work, but worst of all, he chased after every young lady in the county – including myself. I wanted nothing to do with him, but there were others who gave in to his tender words and caresses.

"Vanessa was hardly blind; she saw how Joe flirted with all the others, and it turned out she possessed something of a temper. They'd have terrible fights, and Joe would take off for the village pub again on their one horse.

"Well, on the first Christmas Eve after they were married, Joe came home late from the pub, drunk as usual. Later on the story was that he'd fallen in front of the hearth, hit his head, didn't even know as he was burned alive. But there were many of us who thought otherwise: That your aunt had surely had enough, hit him on the head with something like an andiron, and put him in the fire to concoct that story.

"It worked, too – they couldn't prove a thing against her. Plus, Joe was hardly well liked hereabouts, so the constabulary didn't exactly exert much effort on proving he'd been murdered."

I felt a chill despite the hot tea. My aunt was a murderess? And the crime had taken place in a house I'd been invited to share for the rest of my life? "The house…"

Annie reached out and touched my hand for support. "Did something happen to you there?"

I nodded, ashamed to admit the full truth. "Last night…I was – attacked."

Annie exhaled sharply before saying, "Your aunt was wrong to invite you, and on the very night of the murder, no less. She must have thought she could control him, or that he was weak –"

George entered then, saying he had the carriage ready; he told me he'd come back later in the day with my bags. I thanked the two of them for the great kindness they'd shown me.

Now that I look back on it, I think I can say in all truthfulness that I owe my life – or whatever is left of it – to them.

Elise looked up from the book, dazed. "My God. Well, I suppose we know now why she had to self-publish this.

Sex with a ghost simply wasn't done in 1895."

Ray, who had already broken open a second bottle, laughed and added, "I'm still not clear on whether we're supposed to take this as fact or fiction."

"Oh, Ray, surely…" Elise broke off. She'd been about to say, "It *must* be fiction," but then she realized she wasn't so sure. A memoir about hysteria, perhaps? Wasn't the spiritualist movement in full swing when this written? Perhaps Mrs. Warren had been more deeply influenced by all the stories of ghostly contact than she'd been aware of.

Ray gestured at the book. "Is there more?"

Elise flipped through it. "One more chapter. The rest of the pages are blank – I guess to give it enough heft for the binder."

"Well, let's finish it out, then."

Elise turned the page. "Chapter Four…"

George was as good as his word, and arrived later on Christmas Day with my two bags. There was no train back to Manchester until the 27th, so I spent a quiet Boxing Day in the pub, letting Annie tend gently to my injuries.

A day later I was home again, determined to put it all out of my mind.

A month later I found employment working for an elderly solicitor. The work involved mainly writing letters and keeping accounts, and my employer was benevolent and thoughtful.

In March, I was finally sure: I was with child.

I sat up late into the nights, working out timelines: It *could* be Henry's. We'd been together as man and wife the night before he'd died. I tried over and over to tell myself that was the only logical explanation. Of *course* it was Henry's.

But the pregnancy became increasingly difficult. I knew, of course, about morning sicknesses and the usual little traumas, but that was nothing like what I was going through. Everything, even water, made me violently ill. I was constantly besieged by excruciating abdominal pains. Blood trickled frequently from my womb, staining my undergarments.

My employer not only gave me time away from the job, but provided the best medical care. The doctors were puzzled; they'd never seen such a condition. They asked me if there was any history of problematic pregnancy in my family. I told them I knew very little about my family.

I never confessed what I knew about the father.

At five months, I looked (and felt) ready to burst. I was completely bed-ridden by then, and I'd taken to biting a rolled piece of cloth to prevent shrieking in agony.

Finally, one night in early June, the pain peaked. It was midnight, and I was alone in my bed chambers. I felt a shudder take me, a great deal of warm fluid gushed from between my legs, and the sensation of ten-thousand glass shards piercing me caused me to (thankfully) lose consciousness.

I awoke several hours later, weak but at last out of pain. I struggled to a sitting position, looked down and saw –

I shall never describe what I saw, what had passed from my body as I'd lain unconscious. I was too spent to move, so I waited. The doctor who arrived to check on me in the morning saw the dead thing on the bed and promptly sicked up his breakfast. After, he assured me that he would dispose of it in fire and tell no one what he'd seen.

I was four weeks recovering. Thanks to the careful attentions of my doctors, I did regain my strength. I returned to my work and to my life.

That was some time ago now. I've done my best to put the whole experience behind me, but I've been unable to. I still bear semi-circular scars on the upper part of my body, and I will never conceive again. There've been men who've shown me attention, but I've fled in terror from them. I've never heard from my aunt, although the lovely Lees have corresponded with me throughout the years, bless them. We never speak of Vanessa or of that Christmas.

I know that as much as I try to forget, the rest of my life will be spent re-living that terrible night I spent in the house by the bog, a house where a sprightly yellow paint job and pillows quaintly embroidered with nature scenes couldn't hide a hideous crime and the undying nightmare it had spawned.

Elise closed the book and set it on the table beside the couch. Neither she nor Ray spoke for several seconds.

At last Elise said, "My God."

Ray could only shake his head and gulp wine.

Elise looked down – and her eyes widened at what she saw. "Ray…" She pointed at something beside him on the couch. He picked it up.

It was an ancient satin couch pillow, its sheen faded but still in good condition, hand-embroidered with an image of birds flying over snowy trees.

"This is the house."

Ray picked up the pillow and squinted at it before tossing it aside. "Coincidence…"

"The yellow paint job? The bog? The pillows? Ray, this is *the* house. The one in the story. I'm sure of it."

"That's it—no more ghost stories for you, my darling—"

Elise abruptly stood and went to one of her bags. She'd brought Aunt Priscilla's old family album with her, since she'd thought going through it in her aunt's old home might be a nice small tribute. She found the old, velvet-covered album, stuffed so full of pictures that it bulged out, and carried it back to the light by the hearth. She'd remembered something she'd seen in there, tucked in among all the photos of distant relatives she didn't know—

There. It was a large photo, showing around two-dozen people, dressed in the fashion of the 1930s, three lines on a short flight of steps. There was writing on the back – "*Family Reunion 1935*" – followed by names.

The third name from the right in the top row was "Aunt Jane".

Elise flipped the photo over and peered at the named woman. She was in her sixties, with short gray hair and a flower-print dress. Her expression was the oddest among the group: She seemed to be trying to smile, with a slight tilt to her lips, but her eyes were serious.

Elise showed the writing on the back of the photo to Ray. "There, I knew it: Ray, she's a relative."

Peering at the writing, then the photo, Ray asked (slurring his words), "Who is?"

"Jane – Mrs. H. Warren. The woman who wrote this book."

Ray hiccoughed as he tossed the photo aside. "Don't be absurd, Elise. I'm sure every family in England has an Aunt Jane."

"But I'm sure I've seen mentions of 'Warren' in Priscilla's things, too. We could probably track down the deed history of this cottage to be sure."

"And then what?" Ray staggered to his feet and threw an arm out at the hearth, in an overly-dramatic gesture. "'Ladies and gentlemen, step right up and see where the ghost was murdered'? Shall we charge a pound a ticket, sell souvenir shirts?"

This happened more often than not when they were together: They drank too much until the alcohol led to a fight. Elise hadn't wanted to argue on Christmas Eve, but now there was no escaping it. "Why don't you want to acknowledge that it's at least a possibility? Didn't you say that the man who sold you the book said it was written by a woman who'd lived around here? It's not exactly a heavily-populated region, is it?"

Ray raised his arms over his head. Wiggling his fingers, he began to utter a ghostly wail.

Elise was done. She stormed out of the room, heading down a short hall to the first room she found with a locking door. She entered, flipped a light switch, slammed the door, turned the lock. Outside, she heard Ray continue to utter his ridiculous moans. She regretted having left her phone outside; she could've at least plugged in the earbuds and drowned him out with music. Not Christmas carols, though; she'd had enough of the holiday.

He finally went silent, and she waited. Would he come knocking on the door, drunkenly taunting her? She didn't expect an apology, or even an offer at compromise. That wasn't Ray's style.

She turned to examine the room. It had a soft bed, a fireplace, a small dresser, a rocking chair. The bed covers were only slightly dusty. She pulled them back and saw that the bed was made beneath and seemed surprisingly clean. Outside the room, full night had fallen; she had no idea what time it was.

She turned on a bedside lamp, turned off the overhead, removed her shoes, and fell into the bed. The room spun; she'd had too much wine. She knew the sensation would pass soon, so she waited.

While she waited, she thought about the story. She was sure Jane Warren was family, and that this was the house. At that thought, her heart skipped a beat.

Because if this was the house, then this bedroom...

She started to sit up, but the room whirled around harder. She was afraid she'd be sick, so she forced herself back down. Besides, if she came out of the room now, what would Ray say? He'd surely launch into a fresh round of mockery. No, she wouldn't give him the pleasure.

She waited. The spinning slowed. Time passed. Her thoughts grew muddled. The temperature dropped as night set in; she pulled the musty blankets up over herself, enjoying the warmth they brought.

And sleep arrived.

* * * * *

At some point she was dimly aware that he'd entered the room and settled into the bed beside her. He'd come to apologize after all. He'd realized that he'd been wrong.

He reached for her. His touch was cold. Had he been outside? She wanted to ask him, but she couldn't speak. She was incapable of movement.

His frigid hand pulled her shoulder, hard.

Elise knew, then: The door was still locked. It wasn't Ray.

She struggled against whatever force held her, but it was immovable. Weight settled around her. The bed springs creaked.

No.

She wouldn't let this happen.

Elise gathered every ounce of will power she possessed, forced her mouth open…and screamed.

The power holding her evaporated. She was alone in the bed.

She leapt from it and stumbled up. She heard Ray outside, running to her door, calling her name. She reached the lock, twisted it. The door flew open and Ray stumbled in. "Elise –!"

"Ray." She embraced him, the fight forgotten. She didn't know if they could save their marriage, but right then she knew he was human and real and that she wanted to try.

She hung onto him, looking over his shoulder, wondering if Joe even knew he'd lost, or who exactly had defeated him. Elise didn't believe – *couldn't* believe – that *The Christmas Spirit* had come to her by happenstance.

"Thank you, Jane," she whispered to the woman who had just given her the best Christmas gift of her life.

EXCERPTS

(ONE BY EACH AUTHOR)

THE DARKLING

R.B. CHESTERTON (CAROLYN HAINES)

A good storyteller — **and R. B. Chesterton is quite a good storyteller** — knows to lower her voice when she's talking about ghosts. This author (who writes cozy mysteries under her real name, Carolyn Haines) reaches into the grave for the sepulchral tone in which she narrates **THE DARKLING (Pegasus Crime, $24.95),** a moody tale about a sad town that comes to grief trying to relive its glittering past. During the 1940s, movie stars flocked to Coden, Ala., "where pleasure and vice could be indulged" in peace and for a price at the Paradise Inn. But by 1974, the pretty people are gone, the hotel is boarded up, and the locals have linked their dreams for the town's rebirth to the Hendersons, a golden couple with three golden children. Having restored a grand house and raised hopes they might rescue the Paradise Inn, these California transplants spread more sunshine by taking in a homeless teenager and hiring a live-in tutor. That's how Marie Bosarge ("You can call me Mimi"), the 21-year-old narrator, comes to witness the mysterious events in **this spellbinding tale, offering eloquent evidence that Southern storytelling is indeed a very special art form.**

PROLOGUE

IN THE 1940S, CODEN, ALABAMA was a hideaway for movie stars—an isolated playground tucked among live oaks and the placid bay waters where pleasure and vice could be indulged. When Veronica Lake or Errol Flynn came to play, bedazzled lawmen turned a blind eye to the excesses that ride the coattails of fame. Coden was a backwater with incredible natural beauty, the old Paradise Inn, fitted out for royalty, and silence that could be bought.

No one asked questions.

In the summer of 1974, the hotel was abandoned and the stars had found other, more exotic backwaters. The poor were poorer and the rich were gone.

Like most of the rest of the kids around Coden, I'd grown up on tales of glamour lost. While the past intrigued me, I had a more practical bent. "Mature beyond her years" was the description most often attached to me. Not exactly the attributes of a popular young woman. I didn't care. I was the live-in tutor for the Henderson family, a job I'd held for three months. Only twenty-one and fresh out

100

of college, I found myself in residence in the grandest house in south Mobile County with a family that looked like it stepped out of *House Beautiful.* Berta, the mother, kept the kitchen filled with the scent of home cooking. The children were bright and willing to learn. And Bob, oh, he was a handsome man accomplished as an architect, but also a man who loved his wife and children and never failed to show it. The Hendersons were everything I'd been denied—a perfect family. They brought hope that new prosperity had come to Coden.

My grandmother, Cora Eubanks, and most of the residents, pinned their dreams on Bob and Berta Henderson and the belief that they could bring back what had once been lost.

Coden was a dying community, a left-behind fishing village on the small and placid Portersfield Bay of the Mississippi Sound. Like all towns built around water and a fishing industry, it was remote. Much different from Mobile or even the coastal towns of Mississippi. The families of Coden had been there for generations, a mixture of old French and Spanish with a smattering of Irish and Scot thrown in.

In the summer of 1974, Vietnamese families had begun to move in, a point of controversy amongst the "natives." The Vietnamese War was too fresh, the losses of young men from the area too bitter. Still, whether old line stock or newly arrived Asians, these were fishing families that shared a way of life, a relationship with the water and a sun-up to sunset work ethic.

Not so with the Hendersons, a family of golden blond Californians, as exotic as any of the strange blooms in the garden of Belle Fleur, the showcase home they bought and renovated at the water's edge. They were outlanders. Outsiders. They had wealth, looks, education, and, most telling, different expectations. While they were viewed with suspicion by many, it couldn't be denied that the family brought the promise of better times to come. Bob

Henderson's renovation of Belle Fleur was the first step in his master plan. Seeing the old house restored on the rise of land that led down to the Sound made everyone in Coden feel that better times were coming. Bob's dream of bringing the Paradise Inn back to life was the hottest topic of talk in town that summer.

Even I, working in the bosom of the family, believed that the Hendersons would change the luck of Coden. The old stories, the tales of big bands, rollicking parties, movie stars water skiing—somehow by bringing the Paradise back to life, Bob would bring back the flush times. Instead, the Hendersons opened a door to the past that should never have been unsealed. Their arrival initiated a tragic chain of events and unbearable suffering.

I'd thought never to tell this story. I vowed never to think of it again. I changed my name and left, for who would hire a tutor who'd been on the scene of five grisly murders and continued to claim she saw...what? An evil child? A murdering child? An imposter who moved into the heart of a family with only the goal of murder?

So I refused to talk. Not to reporters or therapists. Not to anyone. At last they left me alone. I found another post with a family in Ocean Springs, Mississippi, and I saw their children through to college and then found another family in Biloxi, and another in Gulfport. My duties moved me farther along the Gulf Coast rim until I hit a little town south of Corpus Christi, Texas, where I baked in the full glare of the Mexicali sun.

At night, I drank. Vodka couldn't keep the memories at bay, but it did dull them to the point that I could sleep. Aside from the brutal murders that haunted my dreams, I worried a point of guilt. What role had I played in the destruction of the Henderson family? What role had my grandmother, Cora Eubanks, enacted?

Such dark thoughts are less terrifying in the heat of the late summer sun. So it is now, in the August of a new decade, the second of a new century, that I've taken on the burden of putting my story on paper. The written word has tremendous power. I hope that by writing this I can...I'm not certain what I hope to accomplish. Put my demons to rest? Warn others? Leave a written legacy that might carry more weight than my spoken words? Or perhaps I'm following in the footsteps of Cora, who once left me a document that was the key to the past.

I only know that the long summer days offer me some comfort from the terrors of the dark. I must write fast. Time is running against me. When I'm tempted to back away from this story, as I often am, I remember that I have seen her. Only last week. As young and innocent as the first day she stepped off the bus at Beauchamp's Grocery in Coden in 1974.

As long as the August sunlight heats the woods and fields of southern Mobile County, I force myself to the task of recounting the events of nearly forty years ago. In the darkness of the night, I drink. When the sun is gone I dare not call forth the images of my past for fear she will sniff me out. She has the acute senses and cunning of a wild animal. And she has no mercy, not for a child or me.

How did she manage to get back to Coden? That's a question I pursue even as I chronicle her story. Annie. Such a simple and beautiful name. There is no word in the English language that can strike such fear in me.

To properly tell her story, I must go back in time. The memories of youth in the 1970s would be wonderful, were it not for the events I must remember. My grandmother was the fulcrum that set it all in motion.

Chapter One
JULY 7, 1974

A WHIPPING SUMMER GUST BLASTED off the water, sending a paper bag skittering across the parking lot of Beauchamp's Grocery. I couldn't see the water from the parked car where I waited with my grandmother but I could smell it. That tang of salt and fish and a wildness from the marsh grass that made me long to get out and stretch my legs in a brisk walk.

"It won't be long," Cora said, patting my leg. "Don't fidget."

My grandmother was a social worker for the Department of Pensions and Security, later renamed Human Resources. Annie had come to her attention when she was picked up on the streets of downtown Mobile. At first it was thought she was a teen prostitute, but Cora claimed she was an amnesiac, a girl with a big imagination, a talent for storytelling, and no one to love her, no memory of where she'd come from or what she was meant to be doing. Cora had a soft touch for mistreated children, but she wasn't in the habit of dragging them home. Annie was different, though. Something about her had tugged at Cora's heartstrings.

I was already working as a tutor for the three Henderson children—a job I'd held since the previous May. In the short weeks of my employment, I had found my place in the family. I taught lessons, but more than that; I was valued and respected as part of the family.

I went to work the day after my college graduation, eager yet also unsure. Now I'd gained my footing, but the addition of another teen gave me concern. Cora would hear none of my worries.

"She's a teenager with no place to turn. Give her a chance, Mimi," Cora said. "You may discover you have things in common."

The things I'd have in common with her would be that I would have another charge to educate. My life with the Hendersons was nearly perfect—I didn't see the need to include another child.

Shifting on the car seat to better see my grandmother, I asked, "Why did the Hendersons agree to take her in?" Most families I knew would never consider harboring a strange child, especially a sixteen-year-old girl who had no memory of who she was or where she'd come from. Annie was the only name she'd give.

Grandma, who I'd grown up calling Cora, believed in the power of love. All of my life, she'd told me how love could heal any wound, patch any hole in a person's soul. Love was her miracle drug.

"The Hendersons have room and plenty of love. Once Annie feels secure, her memory will return. I suspect she's been through a terrible trauma. The doctors believe her amnesia comes from some shocking event or accident. The Hendersons are the perfect family to help her heal. Belle Fleur is the place for her. You'll be a part of her healing, Mimi. Perhaps you, too, will find the experience curative."

I wasn't certain that was true. Even after thirty years as a social worker, Cora wanted to believe the best of people. I was only twenty-one, just out of college, and I knew better. But I said nothing. Cora was a figure beloved in the Coden community. She'd asked the Hendersons to foster Annie, and so they would.

Cora had gotten me the tutoring job, a full time position that required me to use my education degree from the University of South Alabama to its maximum potential. I was the compromise between Bob and Berta Henderson. Bob loved old Belle Fleur, the house of his dreams and the perfect project to show his architectural and renovation abilities. He'd bought the property against Berta's wishes. He'd completed the renovation before she'd consider moving here. Bob wanted the slower pace—and perceived safety—of a small, rural Alabama town to raise his children.

Berta, a California girl through and through, refused to send her children to the Alabama public schools. She was more than a bit horrified by the curriculum, not to mention the prevalence of "portable" classrooms, essentially trailers. Before she'd move from the heaven-on-earth of Cambria, California, to Alabama, she negotiated a live-in tutor, four week-long trips to "cities with culture," an in-home movie theater, and piano and violin lessons for all the children. I was young, unattached, and credentialed in teaching. Though I'd been living with Cora, I also longed for a family, something I found nestled in the brood of blond Hendersons. I felt as if the job had been created especially for me

The three children, Donald, nine, Erin, twelve, and Margo, sixteen, were not spoiled, but they were willful. Donald quickly became my favorite. Erin charmed me with her energy, and Margo challenged me. How would this new child, this orphan, fit into the mix? I wasn't sure this was a good idea.

"The bus is late." Cora frowned. "When I was a young woman like yourself the bus was the only way to get into Mobile. Folks didn't have cars like today. We relied on the bus, and it was on time. I know I sound like a fuddy-duddy, but this whole country is going to hell in a hand basket."

We were only six years past the terrible murder of Dr. Martin Luther King, a man my grandmother revered. His death shook her faith in her fellow countrymen and the basic goodness of America, but she didn't stop trying or believing. Girls like Annie—the abandoned, the thrown away, the damaged goods—this was where she made her mark. America might have lost its way, but Cora knew the steep and rocky path she was meant to trod.

The bus pulled in front of the grocery store on a belch of black smoke. It looked as old and worn as the setting. I was about to step out of the car when a gust of wind caught the heavy Pontiac door and slammed it with vicious force, almost catching my hand.

When I looked up, Annie was standing beside the car. Dark curls batted about her small, pinched face. She was beautiful, elfin almost, and she looked so lost. The word that came to mind was "stray." Like a dog or cat hungry for love and attention. I opened the car door, pushing against the wind that tried to keep me safe inside. She simply stood there, as if she didn't know how to help. At last I got the door open and got out.

I extended my hand. "I'm Marie Bosarge. You can call me Mimi," I told her. "I'm Cora's granddaughter. I'm the tutor at the Hendersons."

She shivered in a gust of hot air, and I realized she was nervous. Her too short dress exposed long legs, lean but shapely. She was sixteen, and she looked starved. She came with only one suitcase, a battered brown thing that had once tried to pass itself off as leather before the surface had been scraped and the cardboard beneath revealed. I picked it up and put it in the spacious trunk.

"Climb in," Grandma ordered. "The Hendersons are waiting."

Annie clambered into the backseat, teeth chattering. Cora turned off the air conditioner and away we went, racing down Shore Road ahead of the storm that brewed to the south. The squall had blown in quickly, as marine gales are wont to do. In the summer, we worried about hurricanes, but the Gulf was empty of the whirling tempests that could wreck a coastal town and kill hundreds with high winds and water.

With the air conditioner off, the car was like an oven, and I rolled down my window for a moment of fresh air. Seagulls cried and cawed, circling the marshy shore. The wind seemed to have confused them because they swooped at the car as if they meant to attack. They were curious birds, but not stupid. The erratic behavior puzzled me.

"What's wrong with the gulls?" Cora asked.

"It's almost as if they're disoriented. Maybe something to do with the storm." I'd spent a bit of time bird-watching, and I'd never seen gulls pursue a car. "Or maybe...blind." They acted as if they'd lost their ability to see.

"Maybe it's the car," Annie said from the backseat.

"They're following us."

It was true. The birds moved down the road with us. To my complete horror, a gull came straight at the car like a missile. I reached over and honked the horn as Cora applied the brakes.

"Good lord!" she jerked the wheel, sending my head banging into the passenger window. In the backseat, Annie slammed against the door. The bird hit the windshield with a bloody smack as Cora brought the car under control and stopped.

I got out quickly and checked the bird, but it was hopeless. The impact killed it instantly. The other birds wheeled and cried, circling above me and the car, but they made no attempt to get closer. I moved the carcass to the side of the road. When I got back inside, Cora's hands shook on the steering wheel.

"I can't believe that happened," Cora said. "I've driven this road my entire life. I've never hit a gull."

"Something was wrong with it," I said. In my family, the death of any creature was cause for grief. I was partial to birds and I'd trained as an amateur ornithologist. I wasn't an expert, but I knew gulls didn't deliberately dive into the windshields of cars traveling fifty miles an hour.

Cora was shaken but tried not to show it. "It had to have been sick. I'm sorry, Annie. I don't want that to spoil your arrival here in Coden."

"I don't believe in omens. At least it was a quick death," Annie said. "It didn't suffer."

I hated it when people mouthed platitudes. A quick death. What did that mean? Annie had no clue what she was talking about, but I wisely kept quiet. Cora was struggling to regain her composure, and I didn't want to do anything that would make it harder for her.

She put the car in drive and we started along Shore Road at a more sedate pace. When I glanced back in the side mirror, I saw a dozen other gulls pecking the corpse. They tore at it with a savage frenzy. Gulls were scavengers, but I'd never seen them feast on a freshly dead comrade. My gaze connected with Annie's in the rearview mirror. She watched me with cool calculation.

"What's wrong?" she asked. She was so calm I could only imagine what hardships she'd endured to gain such composure.

"Nothing." I had no desire to spoil her arrival at Belle Fleur. The Henderson family was waiting, a happy occasion. Cora had planned this for days. The bird's death was unfortunate, but there was no reason to mar the remainder of the day.

"Wild creatures are unpredictable, don't you think?" she asked.

"Seagulls are hardly wild creatures."

Annie broke her gaze from mine. "Will the Hendersons like me?" she asked Cora.

"I'm certain they will. This is a big day for them, too. I've told them all about you."

Out of the corner of my eye I watched Cora put aside her shock and assume her professional demeanor. "All we know," I added. "There wasn't a lot to tell since you can't remember anything about your past."

"They'll be charmed by you," Cora said. "And you will adore them. "

"Will they adopt me?" Annie asked.

Cora hesitated. "We've talked about this, Annie. You're sixteen. That's a bit old for adoption. They may foster you until it's time for college. That would be a wonderful outcome for you."

"Yes," she said.

I couldn't see her expression for her face was hidden behind a blowing strand of dark curls, but her voice sounded less than sure. She merely wanted to be loved, I thought. Who could not love a child so beautiful and damaged?

END OF EXCERPT

BLISS HOUSE

LAURA BENEDICT

"BLISS HOUSE, with its blood-stained history of madness and murder, would scare off most potential buyers, but not interior decorator Rainey Bliss Adams, in Benedict's creepy, solidly crafted supernatural suspense novel. In the wake of the gas explosion in St. Louis that killed her husband and left her 14-year-old daughter, Ariel, badly burned, Rainey moves to Virginia's Blue Ridge foothills to buy the ancestral home that she fell in love with as a child. For Ariel, the nightmare begins in the wee hours after the housewarming party, when she groggily sees what appears to be a spectral young woman fall to her death from the third-floor balcony; the next morning, there's a very real body. Lines between fact and fantastic, past and present, increasingly blur, as Benedict (*Calling Mr. Lonely Hearts*) interweaves the ensuing murder investigation with the chilling story of a young woman kept as a sex slave within Bliss House's walls a generation earlier. The final revelation hits horrifyingly close to home for Rainey."

–Publisher's Weekly

CHAPTER 13

AT FIRST, ARIEL THOUGHT IT WAS her father who awakened her. She lay, eyes wide open, listening hard. Outside the window, the sounds were the ones she heard every clear night: trucks on the distant highway, the crickets in the grass that told her summer was hurrying to a close.

"It's like they're saying goodbye," she remembered once telling her father as they sat together on their darkened patio.

This sound was inside the house. Not rhythmic, but insistent. Someone running. Voices, but not happy ones.

I won't be afraid.

Her father had said he would be there, watching over her. She pushed back the light cotton blanket and slipped into the robe that smelled like flowers. The top of it clung to her body, while the skirt floated behind her, making her feel graceful. *Graceful.* Why hadn't her mother said anything about how much better she was walking? First the cane had gone, and now she had almost no pain at all.

She stepped out into the hallway and looked up to where she thought the sounds had come from. Moonlight filtered through the clerestory windows around the base of the dome, tracing shadows everywhere. Maybe there were people from the party who had stayed behind, hiding upstairs. The idea filled her with a strange mixture of fear and delight just as Jefferson's sudden appearance upstairs had. Could it be him?

The footsteps stopped.

"Jefferson?" Ariel whispered. Her voice was small, but sounded loud to her own ears in the vastness of the hall.

But what if I'm afraid?

Across the gallery, she saw the faint glow of a nightlight beneath her mother's door, and she had an urge to run to her mother's room and climb in bed with her, as she had when she was a very little girl. Back then, her father was always there, his comforting, solid presence balancing her mother's warmth.

She had two choices: to run and hide in her mother's room, or to go upstairs alone. She pushed the thought of the ballroom out of her head. These noises were different. Definitely not children.

Someone else was whispering. She strained to make out the words.

Moving quietly down the hall to the staircase to the third floor, she listened. Someone was moving around up above her. Jefferson hadn't admitted to being in the ballroom, and now she regretted not making him confess. He'd asked for her phone number so that they could text one another. She'd thought at the time he was just being nice. But if he was here, in the night, that was a different matter.

Is he looking for me?

When she put a foot on the staircase, it creaked. She wished she'd brought the flashlight her mother had put in her room for emergencies, but knew if she went back for it, whatever was upstairs might be gone when she returned.

Glancing back out to the gallery, Ariel caught a flash. She hurried back to the railing.

The shimmer came from the third floor, and for a moment she thought it might be a flag of some sort, or a swath of fabric. It shone, but was almost transparent as it quickly took the form of a young woman.

She was older than Ariel, maybe about Jefferson's age, and so thin that her mane of red hair overwhelmed her body. The loose, pale garment she wore looked familiar to Ariel, but she couldn't see it quite clearly. That she was barefoot comforted Ariel somehow. It seemed so normal. Maybe it was someone from the party who had been too drunk to drive home.

The shimmer around the girl didn't reach very far into the darkness, but Ariel could hear men's voices coming from somewhere upstairs. She could tell by the attitude of the girl's body that those voices were making her afraid.

If they're real. If they're not a dream.

The girl leaned back against the railing, a sleeve of her robe— *yes, it's a robe. . . .* the *robe*—hanging over it like a curtain. Ariel could hardly process what she was seeing. It was happening fast, but she couldn't look away. In a blink, the girl had climbed up to sit on top of the railing.

The house was so quiet that Ariel could hear the ticking of the clock down in the hall. Her heart pounded. She thought of those seconds just before her father died, the leaden hush that had surrounded them. Like the universe holding its breath.

Slowly, so slowly, the girl leaned back into the air.

The robe floated like a rain-laden cloud around the girl, and moonlight glanced off of it like tiny flashes of lightning. Her arms were a perfect V. Her mouth and eyes open wide. Knowing. Accepting. She might have been crying out, but the only sound Ariel could hear now was the blood pounding in her own ears. Before she could look away, she saw something else: someone, a man she thought, standing at the railing where the girl had gone over.

Ariel flung herself back against the wall so she wouldn't

have to see the girl hit the ground far below her.

When Ariel awoke on the floor, her head cradled in the crook of one arm, she had a single perfect moment of forgetfulness. But as soon as she felt the worn hardwood beneath her palms, she remembered what had happened. Hardly any time had passed at all. The moonlight was no longer so strong, but dawn was still a long way off. "Mommy," shewhispered. The glow of the nightlight from beneath her mother's door hadn't changed.

What will I say? Was I dreaming?

She willed herself to look.

Standing safely on the second floor gallery, she saw that there was definitely a woman or a girl lying on the big oriental rug below. She was barefoot, and had similar hair to the girl in the robe, but she wasn't nearly as thin and was wearing a tight dress that was hiked to her hips. Even from where she stood, Ariel could tell she wasn't wearing panties. One of her legs was twisted at a distressing angle, and Ariel winced, imagining the pain. But she knew the woman wasn't feeling pain or anything else. She was too still for that. Her eyes were open.

This wasn't the girl she'd seen fall from the third floor. "Button." Again, a whisper. One that she heard clearly.

Ariel looked across the hall to see her father standing just outside her mother's bedroom door.

It can't be you, Daddy.

He mouthed something to her that she couldn't understand and put a shushing finger to his lips.

He had come back!

But Ariel's flush of happiness at seeing him quickly retreated. Her father was dead, and death was all around her now. She turned and ran back into her room, slamming the heavy door. Crawling into bed, she gathered every sheet, every blanket within reach into a nest around her.

For a long time she lay there, shivering, her eyes squeezed shut. Finally, the nighttime sounds from outside her open window overcame her panic, and she buried her face in her pillow to cry until she slept.

END OF EXCERPT

THE DEVIL'S BIRTHDAY

LISA MORTON

The prologue from Lisa Morton's new novella *The Devil's Birthday*, available at <u>Bad Moon Books</u>.

Scotland, Halloween Night, 1785

THE GIRL LEFT THE PARTY just before midnight. No one had much noticed her during the earlier festivities, as they'd burned nuts at the hearth and tried to bite apples hung from strings; she had a scarf pulled up around her head and the lower part of her face, leaving only her oddly gold-colored eyes visible. They paid her no mind when she slipped out the door, away from the warm candlelight of the farmhouse and into the cold October night.

It was Halloween, and parties were easy to find in the Highlands. Young people all over the country were drinking and dancing and telling fortunes tonight. Those who were yet unmarried had dozens of methods that could reveal the names of their future true loves; grandmothers, meanwhile, sat in rockers in the corner and entertained the smallest children with ghost stories.

Most of those attending old MacAvoy's All Hallow's Eve gathering had just spent the season laboring on his farm; many would soon be traveling on, looking for other work with harvest done. The girl in the scarf might have come from her own harvest, looking for work as domestic help; or she might have come with one of the others, who'd drunk enough ale to forget their companion. Being forgotten, however, was not why she left the party.

On Halloween night, there was nothing unusual about unmarried men and women stealing out of the farmhouse. Some went to the lime kiln with a ball of blue yarn, hoping their future spouse would yank the other end once they tossed it in; some went to the kale patch, waiting to see what the root of the plant they pulled would reveal about the character of their intended.

The girl, however, went to the barn. She meant to try a divination that left weaker souls crossing themselves and muttering.

Pulling her scarf tighter around her head and over her face (for the night was already cold, and it grew colder with each passing quarter-hour), she opened the door of the barn, hefting the lantern she carried to examine the interior. It was a small structure – really more of a storage shed – and would serve her purposes ideally.

She crossed to the far door and unlatched it, then threw it back. With both doors now open, she set the lantern down on a barrel and walked to a wall where various farming implements hung from nails. She chose a two-foot wide, round, short wooden tray – the wecht, used in the harvest to separate the grains of oat from the chaff.

Returning to the center of the barn, the girl took a deep breath, tucked her scarf firmly into place, raised the empty wecht in one hand, and called out, "I winnow this corn three times in the name of the Devil, that I might know the name of my husband-to-be." She took the wecht in both hands and mimed throwing grain into the air with it. Then she waited.

It didn't take long. A wind sprang up, rushing through the barn, lifting her heavy skirts and shawl. She set the wecht down and turned to face the door she'd come in through. The wind gained in strength until she was forced to squint against it.

A figure appeared in the doorway, apparently impervious to the gusts. It walked forward, silhouetted by the light from the farmhouse, and the shape was *wrong*. It was too tall for a man, something bulged from the head, and the knees seemingly bent backward.

The girl backed away, toward the lantern. The figure entered the barn, and suddenly the door slammed shut behind it, stopping the wind.

The Devil stepped into the circle of light cast by the girl's lantern. She gasped as she saw his horns – thick, long and curving, like a ram's – his pale skin and glowing eyes, his bare chest and heavily furred legs, with an animal's joints and tall, black hooves. Something hissed behind him, and the tail that swung into view was topped with an open-mouthed, fanged serpent's head.

"Well, lass," he said, grinning, revealing pointed yellow teeth, "so you've called me on Hallowe'en in order to know the name of your husband, eh?"

The girl stared in mute terror, one hand holding her scarf in place.

The Devil walked closer to her, running his eyes over her body. "Are you sure you're wanting to know this? You'd not prefer to find out…the *natural* way?"

The girl shook her head, trying to remain resolute.

The Devil tilted his head back and laughed, a sound that held the crackle of flames and grating brimstone. "Very well, then, girl: The name of your future husband is…THE DEVIL!"

The girl gasped and ran for the barn's back door, but it slammed shut before she reached it. She tried to open it, but it wouldn't budge; she rattled it, putting all of her weight against it, but it remained fixed.

She felt heat on her shoulders, and whirled to see the Devil standing right behind her, leering at her. "You're a fool – you forgot the most important part of this spell: You have to remove the doors from their hinges. Otherwise, I can still close those doors…and you have no way out."

He began to advance on her. She backed away, her eyes wide. He reached out, and she ducked as one claw scraped the air where her cheek had just been. "You're mine, now, lass. Mine until sunrise, although I doubt you'll last that long…"

The girl staggered as her back hit the wall of the barn. Her hand groped frantically around behind her, seeking escape.

The Devil pressed closer, and his musky scent nearly gagged her; the snake-head peered around his side, eyeing her hungrily. "Now, let's see what my All Hallows' bride looks like under all those clothes –"

He broke off as three raps sounded on one of the barn doors. He frowned and listened, seeking the source of the sound. "What…?"

The girl spoke for the first time. "Ah, good – that'll be Father Hume."

The Devil squinted at her. "Father…? What are you playing at, girl?"

The girl reached up and tore her scarf away, revealing a lustrous auburn mane and caramel-hued skin. "Hello, Auld Nick – it's been a while."

The Devil cried out in anger and backed away, his eyes blazing. "Sathariel!"

She cast aside the concealing shawl, revealing both her broad, muscled shoulders and the long sheathed dagger in the belt around her waist. She plucked the dagger free and the blade gleamed in the lantern's light. "Good – I was beginning to think you'd forgotten me. After all, that scarf wasn't really much of a disguise, but apparently you're too arrogant or stupid to see past it."

He tried to remain indignant, but his eyes kept returning to the dagger. "Actually, I hoped you'd given up this nonsense. Our paths haven't crossed in fifty years…"

"I try to find you every Halloween, you old demon, but you've eluded me. A bystander might think you were afraid."

"I'm not afraid, Angel, but I'm also not interested. There are others calling my name who really *are* deliciously foolish humans, so I'll just bid you farewell and I hope you enjoy all the saints on the morrow."

Satan gestured at the nearest door, which opened. He ran for it, moving so fast he was a blur – but he pulled up short at the threshold. He frowned, tried to walk forward, but something barred his way. "What is this?"

"It's what my friend Father Hume was busy with outside while you pranced and gloated. As soon as he knew you'd arrived, he made a circle all the way around the barn with holy water."

Outside, a man in a priest's cassock stepped into view. He smiled and saluted the Devil with a nearly-empty bottle of holy water. Satan spun to see Sathariel behind him, toying idly with the dagger. "I'm afraid it's now *you* who are trapped in here…with me."

The Devil uttered one harsh bark of dismay before turning on Sathariel. "Now, this is just cruel! I'm allowed this one night a year to come to earth – that was the deal I set up with your former Superior, so who are you to get in the way?"

"Yes, you get to come to earth…but that doesn't mean I can't try to stop you from committing mischief, especially the kind that scares young girls half to death."

"Oh, come, now – you know *half* to death is all I can do. I can't even touch them while they're alive. Angels, on the other hand…"

Sathariel groaned, found her abandoned scarf, and picked it up, holding it out. "I've a mind to gag you so I don't have to listen to this all night."

The Devil flicked a wrist in the direction of one of the barn's walls, and a long scythe mounted there flew into his waiting hands. "And I've a mind to cut off your hands if you try it."

Grinning, Sathariel said, "Then try it I will." She leapt

forward.

Satan swung the scythe; it should have cut Sathariel in half, but she'd already leapt to the side, and the long blade whistled through empty air. He tried again, and this time she ducked under the arc, coming up with her dagger. He blocked the blow by bringing the scythe handle down, but Sathariel countered with a kick aimed at one knee. The Devil sprang back, and the kick connected only with air. He suddenly spun, his back to her, and just as Sathariel was about to rush forward the snake's head shot up, its jaw clamping down on the cloth of her blouse. She pulled back and stopped, considering her options. The Devil turned to face her.

"We can go on like this all night, you know," the Devil said.

"Sounds like a fine way to spend an All Hallow's Eve." Sathariel crouched. The Devil ran at her, swinging the scythe.

She stepped aside, and as he ran past she grabbed a pitchfork that was propped against the wall; in one fluid motion, she whirled, raised the tool, and hurled it at her opponent. It struck him in the back and drove him against the far wall, pinning him there. Sathariel ran forward before he could squirm free; she put her weight against the pitchfork and drove it further through the Devil and the barn's wooden wall. He shrieked and writhed, but couldn't escape. The snake went silent and buried its head between his woolly thighs. Sathariel reached back for the scarf, which she wrapped around his face three times, silencing him.

"There," she said at last, "I can endure you until sunrise now, and then Hell is welcome to have you back."

She spotted a length of hemp rope, and wound that around his legs and hands just for good measure, then she found a comfy hay bale and sat back to wait. From outside, Father Hume called out, "Are you all right in there, Miss?"

"Aye, Father, and I thank you for your services, but I've got it under control now."

The priest answered, "Then I'll be on my way now. Might I see you at the mass on the morrow?"

"I doubt it, Father."

She thought she heard him offer a small sound of regret, and then the night was silent again.

Sathariel reached into a pouch at her belt, produced tobacco and a small pipe, filled the bowl and lit it with a straw from the lantern's flame, and settled back to while away the night. After a few puffs, she raised her eyes up and asked, "One sign from You, you know…that's all I ask. Just one nod to let me know You approve, that I'm on the right path…"

There was no response. After a few seconds, the Devil began to laugh through his gag, low and guttural.

"Shut up or I'll cut your throat," Sathariel murmured.

END OF EXCERPT

ABOUT THE AUTHORS

CAROLYN HAINES (R.B. CHESTERTON)

Carolyn Haines is the Harper Lee and Richard Wright award-winning author of the Sarah Booth Delaney Mississippi Delta mystery series. She exercises her dark side under the pseudonym R.B. Chesterton. *The Darkling* and *The Seeker* are both available from Pegasus Books, New York. "The Hanged Man," a short story, is available in digital formats. As a reader/writer, short stories and horror were her first loves. An advocate for animals, Haines founded Good Fortune Farm Refuge in lower Alabama. She cares for horses, cats, and dogs. Find out more at www.carolynhaines.com

LAURA BENEDICT

Laura Benedict's latest novel is BLISS HOUSE (Pegasus Crime), praised as "Eerie, seductive, and suspenseful," by Edgar award-winning author, Meg Gardiner. BLISS HOUSE is the first in a series of supernatural suspense novels set in Virginia. Laura is also the author of DEVIL'S OVEN, a modern Frankenstein tale, CALLING MR. LONELY HEARTS and ISABELLA MOON. Her work has appeared in *Ellery Queen Mystery Magazine*, *PANK*, and numerous anthologies like *Thrillers: 100 Must-Reads* and the upcoming *The Lineup: 25 Provocative Women Writers*. She currently lives with her family in the southern wilds of a Midwestern state. Visit her on Twitter (@laurabenedict) and at www.laurabenedict.com to learn more about her and her work.

LISA MORTON

Lisa Morton is a screenwriter, author of non-fiction books, award-winning novelist, and Halloween expert whose work was described by the American Library Association's *Readers' Advisory Guide to Horror* as "consistently dark, unsettling, and frightening". Her most recent releases are the novel *Zombie Apocalypse!: Washington Deceased* and the novellas *The Devil's Birthday* and *By Insanity of Reason* (co-authored with John R. Little). In 2015 her next non-fiction book, *Ghosts: A Cultural History*, will be published by Reaktion Books. She lives in North Hollywood, and can be found online at www.lisamorton.com.